STAY
with me

A *With Me In Seattle* Novel

KRISTEN PROBY

This book is for the readers. You've wanted more from Seattle, and I just couldn't say no anymore. This is a reminder to never say never, and be careful what you wish for.

books by

KRISTEN PROBY

The Big Sky Series:

Charming Hannah

Kissing Jenna

Waiting for Willa—Coming soon!

The Fusion Series:

Listen to Me

Close to You

Blush for Me

The Beauty of Us

Savor You

The Boudreaux Series:

Easy Love

Easy Charm

Easy Melody

Easy Kisses

Easy Magic

Easy Fortune

Easy Nights

The With Me in Seattle Series:

Come Away With Me

Under the Mistletoe With Me

Fight With Me

prologue

Amelia

"You've got to be kidding me."

I sit and stare at my attorney, watching her thin, painted-pink lips move, but I'm definitely not understanding what the hell she's saying, because I'm pretty sure she just said "your divorce isn't actually final" and that just can't be right.

It can't fucking be right.

"—sorry."

She's folded her hands over my file on her desk and is looking at me with sympathetic, blue eyes.

"I apologize, Pam," I begin and shift in my seat. "You're going to have to repeat that because I think you just said that I'm *not* divorced, and that can't be right."

"That's what I said," Pam replies with a nod. "He contested."

He motherfucking contested.

"I sat in a courtroom two months ago, and a judge granted the divorce. I have signed papers."

"I know," Pam says with a nod. "But because he didn't appear in court, and he wasn't pleased with the settlement amount, his lawyer filed contest papers, and the judge granted it."

"This is bullshit."

"I don't disagree with you."

"I worked for *two years* to make this divorce happen, Pam." Two years of panic attacks. Two years of stress. Two years of worrying, every single day, that this divorce would never happen, after five years of mental and emotional abuse. I'm done.

"I know, I've been with you for those two years."

I sit back and stare at her, struck numb. "What now?"

"Well, you'll have to either go through mediation and reach a settlement between you, or we go to court. Again."

"Jesus," I mutter and rub my fingertips over my forehead, trying to wipe away the headache that seems to be permanently housed behind my eyes. "He's trying to suck me dry. This is just about the money, Pam. He's not trying to keep me, or save a marriage that has no chance in hell of being saved."

"I agree with that, as well." Pam sighs and reads over the letter I received from the court for the third time. "We're going to get this handled, Lia."

"I know." I blow out a breath, determined not to cry. I will not give Vincent Borgen another tear. Ever. "So, what now?"

"I want to have him served with failure to appear papers, and I have a hunch that he'll have you served with lawsuit papers."

"A lawsuit?" I stare at her, again, as if she's grown a second nose. "What in the hell could he possibly sue me for?"

"Oh, about a dozen things, all just to make this process more painful and slow." She leans forward again. "So, here's what I want you to do. Get out of town."

"You want me to leave L.A?"

"Immediately," she says with a nod. "We want him to be served first, and I don't want you to be served at all. In the meantime, I'm going to take care of this here."

"Where am I going to go?" I frown. "I guess I could go to my parents' in Seattle."

"No." She shakes her head. "Your parents' address is on record, and they'll try to have you served there. Go to Seattle if you want, but don't stay with them."

"For fuck's sake," I mutter and go back to rubbing my forehead.

"Okay, I have other family I can call."

"Good."

"This is really bad timing. I'm launching my new makeup brand next month, and all of my meetings are in L.A."

"I'm sorry," she says and finally offers me a small smile. "I truly am. I know this is inconvenient and just mean on his part."

"Typical. He's got a mean streak the size of Texas." I rub my forehead again. "I can't believe I'm not divorced from the jerk."

"We'll get it figured out. For now, go on vacation for a while, and I'll keep you posted as to what's happening here. If I need you to appear, we'll arrange it."

"Okay."

"And, Lia, you will want to postpone the launch of your brand. Making that kind of money when you aren't divorced yet will only complicate things."

"And he could get a cut of it."

"He could."

Mother fucker.

"Understood. I'll be in touch."

I walk out of her office and to my car, where I sit and stare unblinkingly at the traffic driving by.

Did that just happen? Am I dreaming?

I pinch myself and then frown at the pain. Not dreaming.

So, I need to go somewhere. Not to my parents'. I'm certainly not going to stay with my brother. Archer has more women coming in and out of his bedroom than, well, anyone should. Gross.

And my sister, Anastasia, is just getting ready to move to Seattle for her new job. She is way too busy to add this to her plate.

I bite my lip and pick up my phone, remembering what my cousin Jules said the last time I saw her. That if I ever need anything, all I have to do is call.

Here's hoping she meant it.

She answers on the third ring.

"Hello. Oh crap, hold on." She pulls the phone away from her ear.

"Nate, can you take that away from Stella? She could kill herself with that."

I smile, the sound of her voice making me feel a little better.

"Sorry," Jules says. "Toddlers are adorable when they sleep. When they're awake, they're little terrors."

"She's a beautiful terror," I remind her.

"True. What's up, Lia?"

"I need your help." I clear my throat. "I need a place to stay."

"What's going on?"

I fill her in on the divorce, and how I'm suddenly *not* divorced, and how my attorney wants me to lay low for a while.

"I know it's a lot to ask, but I can't stay with my folks, and I don't like the idea of my name being on a lease somewhere. He'll just figure out where I am."

"I never liked him," she mutters, and I can only nod in agreement. "We will figure this out."

"Are you sure? I know you have a lot on your plate, and I don't want to make things difficult."

"Oh, girl, this is not difficult. You get your beautiful self up here, and we will get you settled. I think I already know of a great place, I just have to call Natalie. Oh, and I'll talk Nate out of kicking Vinnie's ass."

"He can kick his ass. I don't have an issue with that."

Jules laughs, and I hear a commotion in the background. "Shit. I have to go. Just text me when you have details."

She hangs up, and I immediately begin making plans to fly to Seattle. Today.

one

Amelia

"Are you kidding me?" I'm standing in the middle of a beautiful home that has views of Puget Sound, an open-concept living room and kitchen, and a freaking *pool* in the backyard. "When you said that you'd find me a place, I didn't expect this."

"Oh, trust me, I'm not kidding," Jules says and nods, like it's no big deal. "Natalie and I used to live here when we were single. Then Brynna and Caleb lived here for a while, but now that they've moved into their place out in Bellevue, it's just been sitting empty."

"Nat and Luke talked about selling," Nate adds. Jules' husband is something to write home about. I can't look directly at him, or I might embarrass all of us by drooling. With his long hair, dark features, and the sleeve tattoos, he might be every woman's wet dream. "But they haven't yet, so it's the perfect place for you to crash for a while."

"And the best part is, your name isn't anywhere on it," Jules agrees as she slips her hand into her husband's, linking their fingers. "You can stay here as long as you need to."

"You've bought me furniture," I point out, still in awe as men carry couches, tables, and beds up the stairs. "This is insane."

"It was empty because Brynna and Caleb moved out," Jules says with a frown. "You can't sleep on the floor."

"You bought me furniture," I repeat as if she didn't hear me.

"You're family," Jules says. "So there's really nothing else to discuss.

Do you want me to have one of Nate's minions bring in groceries?"

"His minions?" I raise a brow, and Jules laughs.

"Inside joke," she says and smiles up at her husband.

"I can make a call," Nate says, but I shake my head no.

"I can call Uber Eats for that, or order with any grocery store and pick it up. The internet is a beautiful thing."

"You're sure? Nate has people." Jules tilts her head, watching me with our signature Montgomery blue eyes.

"Me, too." I hold up my phone for them to see and smile. "Really, I'm great. This is *so great.*" I feel tears threaten, but before they can fall, Jules wraps me up in her slim arms and holds me close.

"I'm so happy you're here. Take time to settle in. Luke's already called to have the internet hooked back up, and the Wi-Fi info is on the kitchen counter." She backs away and bites her lip as she looks around. "I think that's it, but if you need anything, just call. We're not far, and Luke's right up the street."

"Where's Natalie?"

"Oh, she's around too, but she had a baby about six weeks ago, so Luke keeps her tucked away." Jules rolls her eyes, and Nate just grins. "Luke's a little protective."

"That's kind of sweet."

"It's their fourth baby, Lia." Jules shakes her head. "He's turned her into a baby factory."

"They're quite happy," Nate says and then leans in to kiss Jules' cheek. "And Luke insists they're finished at four children."

"*Four* kids?" I ask. How in the world did I not know that they now have four kids? "Wow, I guess I haven't been home in a while."

And that just makes me sad, and angry at Vinnie all over again. I wanted to move home years ago, and he wasn't having it.

"You haven't," Jules says. "But you're home now, and I hope we get to see plenty of you."

"That would be great."

"We should let her get settled," Nate says. "Here are the keys to Julianne's little red Lexus."

"You do not have to give me your car," I insist. "I can rent one."

"It's really no biggie," Jules says. "I don't use the Lexus much anymore because it's too small for Stella's booster seat. It should get driven."

"Thank you. And thanks for letting me crash at your condo for a couple of days."

"It was our pleasure," Jules replies. "But you'll be happier here. It's hard to live with kids that aren't yours."

"Stella is beautiful."

"And a handful." Nate shrugs. "She's four."

We walk toward the door, and Nate stops and looks down at me. The man is *tall*.

"Lock this door, Lia. Always."

"I will." He's so *intense*.

"And set the alarm."

"Yes, sir." I smirk up at him, and he just smiles.

"Typical Montgomery woman, aren't you? Sarcastic as hell."

"Thank you." I drop into a curtsey and make them both laugh. "Don't worry, I'll lock up. But I think I'm fairly safe here."

"You are," Jules says as she waves and they leave, walking out to their black Mercedes SUV. The Lexus is parked in front of them, gleaming in the warm summer sunshine. It's going to be a pleasure to drive that little convertible around town. It takes the sting out of missing my own Mercedes in L.A.

I wave them off and walk back inside, obediently locking the door behind me. I guess if I have to be away from home for an unknown length of time, this isn't a bad place to do it in. It's great to be back in Seattle, where I know my family is just a phone call away if I need them.

Jules and Nate didn't have to buy this furniture. I could have done that, but they wanted to, and now I don't know how I'll repay them.

Not that they want me to repay them.

I shake my head and walk up the stairs to my bedroom. It has a killer view of the water and an en-suite bathroom with a long countertop, which is perfect for all of my makeup. I'll use the other bathroom on this floor to store the deliveries that I receive and to go through and decide which products I want to try and which I want to give away.

My job is fucking amazing.

Just when I get my suitcases unpacked and stored in the guest room, the doorbell rings, and everything in me stills.

Well, everything except my heart, which is beating out of my chest.

"It's just someone at the door," I remind myself. "It's probably not a process server. It's probably just a delivery."

Once down the stairs, I peek out a side window and find a man standing in front of the door. He's tall, with sunglasses covering his eyes. His dark hair is long. Not as long as Nate's, but he could use a haircut.

He's wearing a hoodie in the colors of Seattle's football team, and cargo shorts, which makes me frown.

If he's cold, why is he wearing shorts?

But the most important thing is, his hands are empty.

I open the door, only wide enough for one eye to peer outside. "Yes?"

"Hi." He takes off his sunglasses and offers me a smile. "I'm Wyatt Crawford, your neighbor from across the way." He points to the large, white house behind him.

"Okay."

He tilts his head to one side. "I just saw the furniture being moved in here earlier and wanted to introduce myself."

"Great. Thanks." I move to shut the door, but he stops me.

"What's your name?"

"Look, Wyatt, I don't have any sugar or flour or extra eggs."

"I'm not baking."

"And I don't want any cookies."

"Not selling."

"And I don't need to find Jesus."

"Last I checked, He wasn't lost."

Okay, that makes my lips twitch, but I hold firm.

"Thanks for coming over to say hi. I have stuff to do." And with that, I shut the door and lock it. I lean my back against the wood and shut my eyes. I'm not a rude woman. But I am unnerved, and my guard is up, and

I'm here alone.

Not to mention, I don't trust men.

I peek out the side window to see Wyatt walking down the driveway toward his house, and I head back upstairs, ready to get my makeshift studio set up in the guest bedroom.

I may not trust men, but the neighbor is handsome. Not that I'm in the market for a handsome man—or any man for that matter.

"IF TODAY'S VIDEO helped you, please give it a like below, and don't forget to click that subscribe button to be a part of the Beauty Brigade, my friends. I'll be back next week with something new. Before I see you again, remember that the most beautiful part about you is what's inside of you. We're just polishing up the outside. Have a great week, everyone."

I smile as I hit end on the camera and sit back to look through the video to make sure there's nothing that I need to film over again.

I'll splice it together tomorrow and get it ready to publish on YouTube on Friday.

I've made quite the name for myself as a beauty and fashion vlogger. With more than three million followers on YouTube, and close to two million on Instagram, I have an impressive following.

All because I love makeup and pretty clothes.

I've been told that the camera loves me, which is a bonus.

Now, I've been approached by one of the biggest makeup and skincare retailers in the country to formulate my own makeup brand. It's almost ready to launch, but I'm stuck in this holding pattern. Again.

I thought it was over. I thought I could finally move forward with my life and leave my past where it belongs.

Instead, I'm waiting. Just like I have been for more than two years.

It's ridiculous.

I shake my head as I wrap up the video, turn off the lights, and carry my makeup brushes into the bathroom to clean them and get them ready for the next recording.

The doorbell rings, and I roll my eyes, hopeful that Mr. Neighbor hasn't decided that he needs a cup of sugar, after all. But it's not Wyatt, it's the UPS man with a delivery.

Day one, and the deliveries have already caught up to me. Which is fantastic.

I unbox the goodies from It cosmetics, and log the foundations, powders, and brushes into my spreadsheets. I keep track of everything that arrives, whether I've ordered it or if it's a freebie from the company. I also keep track of if I try it, use it in a video or on Instagram, and what I think of the product.

With dozens of things arriving each week, there's just no other way to keep track of everything. Not to mention, it feeds my organized soul.

My phone pings with a text from Jules.

If you're free, I'm bringing Natalie and wine over at 6pm. Sit by the pool?

I grin, excited to see them both, and reply. *Yes! Yay! I'll order pizza.*

I check the clock. I have two hours until they arrive. It's the perfect amount of time to get in some yoga and a shower.

Just as I'm about to step under the hot spray, Jules texts back. *Awesome. See you soon!*

"I HAVEN'T TOLD my parents that I'm here yet," I confide to Nat and Jules a few hours later. We're sitting by the pool in the backyard, lounging on the most comfortable outdoor chairs I've ever sat in, sipping our wine.

We've already decimated the pizza.

"They won't be happy," Jules says, exchanging a look with Natalie, who looks fucking amazing for just having had a baby.

"I know." I sigh, watching the water in the pool. "It sucks. My family has been under enough stress because of my divorce. I finally thought it was over, and we all celebrated. With a party. How do I say *'oops! Never mind!'"*

"I wouldn't say it like that," Natalie replies with a laugh.

"I know for a fact that Uncle Stan and Aunt Sherri would be totally supportive and angry on your behalf." Jules takes a sip of her wine.

"I know. I'll call them tomorrow." I fidget with the button on the cushion of my chair. "Thanks for everything, Jules."

"You've thanked me about forty times."

"Well, I'm thanking you again. And you, too, Nat. Thanks for letting me stay here. It's so beautiful, and perfect for what I need. I set up a studio in the upstairs guest room for my videos."

"Oh, perfect," Nat says with a smile. She might be one of the most beautiful people I've ever met. With long, dark hair, green eyes, and a calm soul, she's always made me feel comfortable around her. "I want you to be at ease here. Well, as at ease as you can, given the circumstances. And if you need anything, Luke and I are just up the road a ways."

"Thanks." I blow out a breath. "Honestly, I'm a bit surprised that you're both so willing to help. Not because I think you're mean or anything, but, Jules, you're a bit older than me, and we've never been close. I always looked up to you."

"Well, when I was twenty, and you were fifteen, I probably didn't want you around," Jules admits with a laugh. "But you're an adult, and you're my cousin. I'm always happy to help. I would love to see more of you. I think we have a lot in common."

"I watch your videos every week," Natalie adds. "I get a lot of great tips from you."

"Me, too," Jules says with a nod. "We're girly girls, through and through."

"I love that," I reply. "I'd love to go shopping with you guys."

"Hallelujah," Natalie says, throwing her hands into the air. "I've been pregnant forever, and now that Chelsea is a couple months old, I can leave her for a few hours at a time. So, yes. Please, let's go shopping soon."

"We could invite all of the girls," Jules says, her brain working. "Make it a shopping day-slash-girls' night out."

"Oh, yes," Nat says, nodding vigorously. "You probably haven't had a chance to get to know everyone."

"I haven't been home since Dom's wedding."

"That was three years ago," Jules says. "We definitely need to get all the girls together."

"Awesome." I high five both of them, excited to spend time with all of my cousins and their significant others "Hey, I've been meaning to ask, what's in that building?" I ask, pointing to the small structure behind the house.

"My studio," Natalie says. "Just so you know, I'll be in and out sometimes with clients, but we'll walk around the house. I take photos in there."

"Oh, how fun."

"I should do some photos for you," Nat says. "You're absolutely stunning."

"She does boudoir photos," Jules warns me.

"Actually, I could use a bunch of shots for my new brand. I can't be in L.A. for the sessions, but I bet we could do them here."

"I'd be happy to," Natalie says, her face lighting up with a smile. "Just let me know what you need, and we'll make it happen."

"Thank you. I could also use some shots for social media. I had a girlfriend in L.A. who did those for me, but—"

"Say no more," Natalie says, holding up a hand. "I'm your girl, and I'm ready to get back to work part-time. Let's set something up for later in the week."

"This is amazing." I stare at both of them as they smile back at me. Wide, happy smiles. It feels so good to be back with family. "I can't wait."

"Me either," Natalie says.

"I want to come, too," Jules adds.

"I wouldn't have it any other way."

two

Wyatt

S o, she wants the cabinets on the other side of the kitchen. I stare at the blueprints and scowl.

There isn't even a fucking *wall* there.

My phone rings at my elbow.

"Yeah."

"What has your panties in a twist?" My brother, Jace, asks on the other end of the line.

"Difficult client," I reply and drag my hand down my face before looking out my office window, which faces the mysterious woman's house just across the street. Another delivery truck has pulled up, and just ahead of that, a dark-haired woman climbs out of her luxury SUV, along with a young couple.

What the hell is going on over there?

"Did you fall asleep?" Jace asks.

"Sorry, what did you say?"

"Levi and I are going to the Celtic Swell for dinner. Do you want to go?"

The ocean-front bar isn't far from my house. "Sure. What time?"

"Six," he says. "You sound like you could use a beer."

"Or five," I say with a sigh. "Sorry, this client has been a pain in my ass. She wants me to completely rearrange the kitchen, but where she wants the cabinets, there is no wall."

"Hard to put cabinets against thin air."

"Exactly." I watch in fascination as the delivery truck leaves, and my smiling neighbor carries a huge box inside the house.

"So, what's new?" Jace asks, clearly not in a hurry to hang up.

"I have a new neighbor."

"That's boring as fuck," he replies, and I can almost hear him rolling his eyes. "Have you gotten laid lately?"

"When do I have time for that?"

"That's my point."

"You have a point?" I scowl at my phone. "You're not making any sense."

"My patient just arrived. I'll talk to you at six."

He hangs up, and I stand in the window, watching the happenings across the street. What in the world is going on over there?

And why am I so intrigued by it?

Okay, that's a dumb question. Neighbor Girl is sexy as fuck, and as Jace pointed out, I haven't gotten laid in more than a minute. She said all of six words to me, and I thought she was adorable.

What I could see of her.

I shake my head and turn back to my drafting desk, doing my best to forget about *her* and focus on this task.

How the fuck do I put cabinets where, clearly, there is no place to *put* cabinets? Without rearranging the whole blueprint, that is.

I bite my lower lip and stare at the paper until it's all blurry, and then decide, screw it.

I'll go for a run.

I change clothes, put on running shoes, and walk out the front door to see another delivery truck parked across the street, and my neighbor struggling with one of the boxes.

I jog over and smile at her, finally getting a good look at her, and holy fuck, she's beautiful. Long, light blond hair frames a face that might have been created by the gods. She's petite, with the bluest eyes I've ever seen in my damn life.

"Hey, can I help?"

"Oh, no, I've got it." But she fumbles, and the box ends up on the ground just as the delivery guy pulls away from the driveway. "Or, I don't."

I pick it up and blink in surprise. "It's heavy. Do you have a body in here?"

"You'll never know," she says with a smirk. But as I start to walk in the house, she blocks me.

"Wait, I don't know you."

"Yes, you do, I'm your neighbor. Wyatt. Remember?"

"No, I mean I don't *know* you. You could be a serial killer for all I know."

I raise a brow. "You're the one with the heavy box that might well have a body inside, and I'm the killer?"

Her lips twitch, and finally, I get to hear her laugh. It's wonderful. Warm and husky, and she shrugs good-naturedly.

"I swear, I'm not a serial killer," I assure her.

"Thief?" she asks and bites her lip, her eyes twinkling with humor.

"Not unless you count when I was six and lifted a candy bar from the drug store."

"So you live a life of crime, then." She sighs dramatically, and I immediately love her sarcasm. "Fine, you can come in."

She leads me inside. Her ass is tight in her little denim shorts, and her blond hair is long, falling down her back almost to that perfect backside.

My cock just came to life.

"You can just put it on the dining room table." She gestures to the table already covered with other boxes and mail.

"Where?"

"Hmm." She taps her full lips with her finger, then shifts a few boxes, making room for me. "There."

I set it down and step back to take in the space. Aside from the table, it's tidy.

"Good, because this sucker is heavy. I'm guessing an ex-boyfriend?"

"That's right," she says and hooks a strand of hair behind her ear, smiling widely, and then her gaze falls to my arm. I can't help but give it a little flex, just to watch her eyes dilate.

So, the attraction is mutual.

Good to know.

"Do you need anything else moved?" I ask her and watch her shake herself out of a daydream.

"No. Thanks. Sorry."

"Why are you sorry?"

She laughs and pushes her fingers through her hair, shaking her head. "I don't know. I appreciate your help. That was a heavy one."

"What is all of this stuff?"

Her eyes suddenly go cold, and I know I've lost her. "Thanks for the help," she says again, dismissing me.

"My pleasure. Before I leave, what's your name?"

"Lia," she replies, not saying any more, and I consider that a win. I nod and leave her house, jogging down to the waterfront.

One of the reasons I love this neighborhood is because it's safe enough to run any time of day, and I jog to clear my head.

There are miles and miles of sidewalk that wind along the coastline, and I can watch the boats sail on the choppy, blue water. People are walking dogs, pushing strollers, sitting on blankets.

There are always people.

I reach over my head and pull off my t-shirt, ball it up in my hand, and focus on the steady pounding of my feet on the pavement.

And before long, my mind empties, and I can just enjoy the sun and the salty air.

"WHY THE FUCK do you have a porn 'stache?" I ask Levi, my oldest brother.

"Because he's going to do porn," Jace says and earns the death glare from Levi, making him laugh.

"The cop thing not working out?" I ask him with a straight face and take a sip of my beer.

"Fuck both of you," Levi replies. "I like it."

"It's awful," Jace says. "But, if the porn 'stache thing draws in the ladies, who am I to judge?"

"It's just a regular mustache," he insists. I sit back and study him. He's in his late thirties, with a little grey making its way through his dark hair. I figure it's the job that's done that to him.

Being a detective in a city the size of Seattle isn't for the faint of heart. "Stop harassing him," I say to Jace. "Did you open anyone up today?"

"Two," he says with a nod. Jace is one of the top cardiovascular surgeons in Seattle, and at thirty-six, that's impressive. "And I saw seven others in my office. It's going to be a busy week. What's up with you, Wyatt?"

"I have a new neighbor," I reply because that's the newest thing happening right now. "Yes, I know. You're saving lives, Levi's catching bad guys while seeking a career in porn—"

"I'm not doing fucking porn."

"—and I have a new neighbor. Fascinating. Except, it kind of is. She's mysterious."

"How so?" Jace asks.

"Well, she gets deliveries all day long. And other people come and go, some couples and some singles."

"Brothel," Levi says immediately, making me laugh, spitting out my drink.

"I don't think so. Oh, and when I went over there a few days ago to introduce myself, she only opened the door wide enough for me to see one eye."

"Creeper," Jace says, and I shake my head.

"No, she seemed nervous."

"Brothel," Levi repeats, making me smirk again.

"I helped her with a heavy delivery today, but there's nothing odd about the inside of her house. She seems pretty normal, just private. She doesn't come and go. I've never seen her leave the house, now that I think about it."

They both frown. "Maybe she's agoraphobic," Levi suggests.

"Or she might have that disorder where she's allergic to the sun," Jace adds. "So maybe she leaves at night."

I'm blinking, watching both of them with a frown on my face. "Why are you both so fucking dramatic?"

"What?" Jace demands. "If she's not leaving the house, and has things delivered, it makes sense that she *can't* leave the house."

"So, what's up with all of the people coming and going?" I ask. "I could have sworn I saw Will Montgomery, as in the quarterback, over there the other day. And the movie star, Luke Williams, if I'm not mistaken."

"Have you had a fever?" Jace asks, and I flip him off.

"Friends?" Levi suggests. "Business?"

"Maybe she's a celebrity call girl. Is she hot?" Jace asks and then throws his head back and laughs when I just stare at him. "Of course, she is. *This* is why you're so curious. Just go over there and talk to her."

"I did, and she wasn't interested in talking."

"Well, maybe she'll just remain a mystery," Levi says with a shrug. "Look at that, Jace, our baby brother finally met a woman that he can't charm."

"Just don't turn into the perv across the street who watches her every move," Jace says. "You're better than that."

"I don't watch her every move," I reply and roll my eyes. I just watch her moves when I catch glimpses of her from my office, which does not make me a pervert. "I'm just curious."

"So, on a scale of Mom to Blake Lively, how hot is she?" Levi asks.

"Fuck you."

"Hotter than Blake?" Jace asks, stunned. "Whoa. I'd be obsessed, too."

"I'm not fucking obsessed."

I'M PULLING INTO my driveway just as Lia pulls into hers. I'm surprised. Maybe she *does* only leave the house after dark.

Which is ridiculous, but here we are.

I step out of my car and see her looking over at me, so I wave. She smiles and waves back before disappearing into her house.

My phone is ringing as I unlock my door. I cringe at the caller I.D.

"Hello, Mrs. Malkowitz."

"Hello, dear," she says. I regret taking this job. Yes, it's bringing in close to a million dollars, but it's also bringing me anxiety and calls at ten in the evening from the homeowner. "Thank you for sending over the changes to the kitchen today."

"You're welcome."

"I hate it."

I sigh and drag my hand over my face. "I'm sorry to hear that."

"I really think we should just go back to the way it was at the start."

Of course, you do. I wonder how far away my drafting pencil is. Because I'd like to stab my own eye out in frustration.

"We can certainly do that," I reply calmly. "Is there anything else I can do for you?"

"Oh, no, that's all. I wanted to get back to you right away."

I check the time. I sent those plans over seven hours ago. All I can do is laugh as I say goodnight and end the call.

I'm *so* ready for this day to be over.

"YOU JUST SIT right there," Lia says and winks at me. There's a stage in her living room—with a pole—and I'm sitting on a lounge chair, watching her. "This was in the box you brought inside. I wanted to surprise you."

"I'm surprised," I reply. She smiles and turns away from me, slowly peeling her clothes off. When she turns back to me, her shirt and bra are gone, but her long, blond hair covers her tits. "Do you want to see these?"

"Hell yes."

"Not yet," she says with a laugh. "I want to tease you."

"It's working." My hands flex in and out of fists as I watch her dance around the stage, stripping out of the rest of her clothes but not showing me her breasts.

She even starts to dance around the pole, managing to keep her nipples covered.

"Watch this," she says and effortlessly climbs the pole, swinging around it gracefully. "I'm really good at this."

"I'm not complaining."

She whips her legs up over her head and then stomps to the floor, making a loud bang.

Over and over again, she stomps her feet on the stage, until I finally wake up.

My cock is hard in my hand, and I'm swiftly working myself up to an orgasm when I realize that the banging isn't from my dream.

Someone is pounding on my damn front door.

I climb out of bed and reach for my boxers, immediately thinking of spaghetti, baseball, *anything* to get rid of this boner.

But then I open the door and come face-to-face with the source of said boner.

three

Amelia

"Oh, so you've got jokes," I say to my cousin, Will. He's snickering behind his hand, and his wife, Meg, just rolls her eyes. "Hey, you're going to eventually need those."

I stare at the box of condoms he just dropped into my Louis Vuitton handbag and cock an eyebrow. "Really? Who, exactly, am I going to screw while I'm being held hostage in Natalie's house?"

"You could meet someone," Will replies with an unconcerned shrug. "And when you do, you'll be safe."

"Now I remember why I didn't come home often," I mutter and shake my head, but Will just smiles again and stands to walk me out of their house. I came over for dinner and to see their sweet little baby, Erin, who has since gone to bed.

"You missed me," Will says and wraps me in his big arms. Will is a *big* man. As the starting quarterback for Seattle's football team, I guess he needs to be. But then, all of the Montgomery men are big. "And if you need anything at all, we're here. Just call."

"I will. You've all done so much already."

"It's what the Montgomerys do," Meg says with a smile and offers me a hug, as well, even though I don't know her nearly as well as I'd like to. "They swoop in and take care of the people they care about."

"Sounds about right," I reply with a nod. "Thanks for dinner. And for letting me vent."

"And for the condoms," Will adds with a wink as I walk out the door.

I just wave and climb into Jules' little car, then zoom down the freeway toward the house that I'm quickly beginning to think of as mine.

I love my condo in L.A. My car, my friends, my life. But then I come here, and this fits, too. It's damn confusing.

I mean, I could work from Seattle, right?

No. Probably not.

I sigh as I turn off the freeway and follow a Lexus SUV into my neighborhood. I'm surprised to see that it's my neighbor from across the street. What did he say his name is? Wayne? Wesley?

Wyatt. Pretty sure it's Wyatt. Which is sexy all by itself. But then when you add in the muscles he was sporting when he helped with my boxes, and the freaking sleeve tattoo to go with them, well . . . I might have salivated.

I park and climb out of the car and offer Wyatt a wave before I walk inside to crash. It's been a long day. Natalie came over to take photos for my social media this week, and while it was super fun, changing clothes every twenty minutes, tweaking my makeup, choosing new accessories for each shot, was freaking exhausting.

And then Will made me laugh for two hours, and my stomach got a killer workout.

My family is funny. They're also wonderful, and I've missed them more than I realized.

I have makeup brushes to clean and put away before bed. I always clean my brushes after every use. Getting an infection from bacteria is my worst nightmare.

Speaking of nightmares, I sigh when I take in the sight of the staging bathroom with makeup and brushes strewn over the entire countertop.

"What a mess." I sigh and begin to organize. My mind empties, and before long, the mess is cleaned up. I wash my face, then change into a tank top and clean panties, and rather than watch TV or other beauty vloggers' videos, I simply climb into bed and let my body fall into an exhausted sleep.

THE BEEPING WON'T stop. Actually, beeping isn't a good word.

Chirping. That's a good word.

I've stomped all over this godforsaken house, trying to track down the source of the noise, but it's not here.

Yet, it *is* here.

And that doesn't make any sense at all.

I prop my hands on my hips and tilt my head, listening.

Chirp. Five seconds go by. *Chirp.*

What the hell?

I can't sleep like this. I pace around the kitchen and then march to the front door, throwing it open and listening.

The chirping is louder.

It's coming from Wyatt's house, and it needs to stop, *now.*

So I take off, no shoes, no clothes, marching to his front door on a damn mission. It's a warm summer night, with a light breeze that actually feels great on my warm skin.

I bang on his door and look around. No lights on in the houses on the street. His car is in the driveway, so I know he's home. I mean, it's the middle of the night, so where else would he be?

I bang again. If he's sleeping, which I can't imagine how he could through that noise, he can just wake up and deal with me. I may sound irrational right now, but damn it, a girl needs to sleep.

Finally, he yanks the door open and glares at me with shining hazel eyes.

"What is that noise?" I demand.

"You. *You* are the noise." His chest is heaving. His naked, slightly hairy, very sexy chest. Not to mention, his light brown hair is a mess, and his chin is stubbled, and his tattoos are just . . . *yum.*

"There's a chirping," I insist, trying to ignore the fact that he's only wearing short boxer briefs. The kind that clings to a man's ass and shows off his thighs.

And, you know, other things. Like the generously sized dick outlined in the cotton.

Holy hell.

"I don't hear anything."

I scowl and pause, listening. Sure enough, it's gone.

"Come on." I grab his hand and pull him behind me. I can hear the door shut. "You have to hear this."

"It's two in the fucking morning," he says but doesn't pull away from the grip I have on his wrist. "Can't this wait?"

"No, because I *can't* sleep." I pull him into my house and shut the door, then hold my hand up. "Stop. Listen."

Chirp.

"See!" I push my finger into his firm chest, and then back up a step so I'm not standing so close to his sexiness. Because I seriously want to attack him.

"So change the battery in the smoke detector." He shrugs and turns to leave, but I run in front of him and block the door.

"I've looked for it *everywhere,* Wyatt. It's not in this house."

He frowns. "Well, it's not at my house."

"Please, help me." I bite my lower lip and watch as he pushes his hand through his already messy hair and feel my nether regions immediately sit up and take notice.

"Can you put clothes on?"

"I'm wearing clothes." I roll my eyes and lead him through the living area, the kitchen, and out to the backyard. "Where is the chirping coming from?"

"You don't have a robe you could put on?"

I turn to frown at him. "You're only wearing underwear."

"Yeah, because it was the only thing I had time to pull on when you were banging my door in."

I swallow hard, the image of a very naked Wyatt suddenly front and center in my brain. "You mean, you sleep naked?"

"Don't you?"

I hold my hands out to my sides. "No, I sleep in this."

"Might as well be naked," he mutters and props his hands on his hips. "I don't hear anything."

"Wait." I hold up a finger and listen, and sure enough. *Chirp.*

"It's in there!" I run over to the studio and open the door, flip on the light, and it happens again. "I found it!"

"Are you running a brothel here?" Wyatt asks, catching my attention. "Or making porn?"

"Excuse me?"

"Or operating a sex club?" His eyes are pinned to the large bed in the middle of the space, the beautiful chaise lounges, and a dining table and chairs. His gaze moves to a rack full of costumes.

"Uh, no."

Chirp.

"Would you please make that stop?" I ask. Wyatt snags a chair and stands on it to pull the smoke detector down to pop out the batteries. His body is long and lean, the muscles ridiculous. Summer is just starting, and he already looks tan. His mussed-up hair is begging for my fingers.

And the tattoos on his arm do things to me. Sexy, crazy things.

"There. You can replace these tomorrow."

"Thanks."

"Back to my question."

"Why do you think I'm running some kind of sex show here?"

He laughs and glances around again, then shrugs. "Oh, I don't know, it might have something to do with all of the sexy stuff in here, and the fact that people come and go from your house all the time."

I take a look around the room and then chuckle. "Maybe I'm just popular, and I don't like to leave the house?"

"Agoraphobia? Allergy to sunlight?"

I laugh and leave the studio, then march back into my house and feel Wyatt on my heels.

"Come on, you can tell me."

"Why do you care?" *I so don't want to tell him all about my personal life.*

"Call me curious."

"Well, curious, I'm not running anything at all to do with sex here." I lean on my countertop and fold my arms over my chest. "The studio out there is my cousin's, and she takes boudoir photos for a living."

"Ah," he says with a nod. "You lease it out to her?"

"No. I'm renting the house from *her.*"

"I see."

"All of these questions are annoying."

His eyebrows climb into his messy hairline in surprise, and I can't help but smirk. "And sexy."

"Which is it? Annoying or sexy?"

"Annoyingly sexy." His lips twitch, and I admit, I want those lips on me. Everywhere. Right now. "Are you attached to anyone, Wyatt?"

He crosses his arms over his chest, mirroring me. "No. You?"

I shake my head no and push away from the counter, walking slowly toward him. I've never done anything like this in my life, but damn it, *look at him.* I'm a grown-ass woman. With needs. I can fuck whomever I want.

"What's your name?" he asks, surprising me.

"I told you it was Lia the other day. Did you forget already?"

"No, your full name." His arms are still crossed over his chest, and his eyes are almost green now as he watches me intently. "What is Lia short for?"

"Amelia," I reply.

"Beautiful name for a beautiful woman," he murmurs, letting his arms fall to his sides.

"Thank you." I feel myself softening toward this man, and I barely know him. "Thank you, by the way, for coming to my rescue tonight. I'm sorry for dragging you out of bed."

"It's okay," he says with a half-smile that sets my blood moving hotter through my veins.

"I'm going to touch you," I say, not meaning to say it out loud, but now that I have, what the hell.

His eyes narrow. "If you touch me, I'll touch you back."

"Man, I hope so."

"I didn't have time to tuck condoms in my underwear," he says, making me laugh, and I immediately send a telepathic *thank you* to Will as I reach for my bag and pull out the condoms.

"I have it covered."

"Was I a sure thing?" he asks.

"I'll explain later." I toss the box onto the counter and leap into his arms, wrapping my legs around his waist and plunging my fingers into his thick hair. He spins, pins me against the wall, and his mouth takes over, claiming mine.

His lips are smooth and sure, working my mouth like a musical instrument. He's thorough. I don't think I've ever been kissed like this.

His hands are cupping my ass, holding me up, but I want them all over my body.

"Countertop," I murmur breathlessly against his mouth.

"Bossy little thing, aren't you?"

I grin. "I want your hands free so you can touch me."

"Can't argue with that." He carries me effortlessly to the kitchen island and sets me down carefully, pulling my ass to the edge so he can prop his crotch, and his hard cock, against mine. "Your pussy is hot."

"So damn turned on," I reply, pulling him back to me. He buries his face against my neck, licking and biting and sending me into crazytown. "You're good at that."

"Just wait, sweetheart." He quickly reaches for the box of condoms, grips it in his teeth, and lifts me, carrying me to the living room. He lays me on the couch and lets the box fall to the floor. "Now I can reach all of you." He pulls my panties down and buries his face in my core, showing me exactly what his magical mouth can do.

And holy fucking hell, it's magical indeed.

I arch my back, my hands gripping his hair, and cry out as the first orgasm washes over me, leaving me breathless.

"So fucking beautiful," he mutters, kissing the insides of my thighs and up my stomach to drag his tongue over my navel. He grips the back of my tank in his hands and simply rips it apart, tugs it down my arms, and throws it over his shoulder. "They're already puckered for me."

Holy shit, the things this man says! I don't know him, and sleeping with strangers isn't my M.O., but there's something about Wyatt that makes me want to throw caution to the wind.

Or burn it altogether.

"Your mouth is incredible." He's wreaking havoc on my breasts. I'm scissoring my legs, silently begging him to fill me.

"What do you need?" he asks against my jaw.

"You, inside me," I reply immediately, tugging his Calvin Klein's down with my feet. "Right now."

"Thought you'd never ask." He reaches for the condoms and makes quick work of suiting up. He grips my hips and moves to flip me over, but I shake my head no.

"I want to watch you," I say, and his eyes narrow. *I do* not *want him looking at my ass.*

Vinnie told me I had a fat ass all the time. This moment is too sexy to worry about what Wyatt thinks of my ass.

He spreads my legs wide, propping one foot on his shoulder and staring down at me with glowing eyes. "Are you sure, Amelia?"

"So fucking sure."

He's gripping his cock firmly, and we both watch as the head disappears into my wetness. I sigh and then gasp when he pushes farther, filling me up.

I haven't had sex in close to three years, but I'm pretty sure it's never felt like this.

"God, you're tight, baby." He leans down, bracing himself on his elbows. "I want to go fast, but I don't want to hurt you."

"This doesn't hurt," I reply and turn my head so I can kiss his wrist. "Not at all."

He clenches his eyes closed and begins to move in earnest, his hips thrusting faster and faster, pushing harder. My legs are wrapped around his waist, tightening, needing him *deeper.*

"Wyatt," I grind out. "Jesus, I'm going to come again."

"Yes." He sucks my nipple into his mouth, and that's it. I come undone, bucking against him. I can't feel my fingers or toes. I don't remember the last time I felt so . . . *good.*

He cries out and succumbs to his own orgasm, every muscle in his fantastic body tensing. I can't stop touching him.

Finally, he pulls away, kissing my nose, then my forehead, and smiles down at me. "Bathroom?"

"Down the hall."

He walks off, and a few seconds later, I hear the toilet flush. Once I've caught my breath, I sit up and rub my hands over my face. I just fucked a stranger.

And it was bloody amazing.

"Are you okay?" Wyatt asks when he comes back to the room. I peer up at him, pulling my hands away from my face, and smile.

"I'm better than okay."

"Good." He smiles and cups my face in his big hand before leaning in to kiss me gently.

"Thanks for coming over," I say, knowing that it sounds lame, but I don't have any idea what else I should say in this situation. I stand and gather my things. "I'll sleep for sure now."

"You're kicking me out?"

"Yeah." I turn back to him and shrug. He can't stay the night. "This isn't a sleepover."

"Give me your phone."

I narrow my eyes at his bossiness but stand and throw on my panties and top, then walk to the kitchen to retrieve it and pass it to him. He raises a brow. "Unlock it, please."

I bite my lower lip and press my thumb to the home button, then pass it back. Wyatt taps on the screen before giving it back to me.

"I may not be staying tonight, but I *will* see you tomorrow."

"Look, this was just—"

"What, Amelia? It was just what?"

"We fucked." I shrug and then feel shitty at the sound of the words. Because I don't know if that's all it was. "And it was fun."

"We fucked," he agrees. "I was already intrigued by you. You can bet your perky little ass that I want to know more. So unless you already hate me, I'll be seeing you tomorrow."

"I don't hate you," I reply and smile softly. He scoops me up into a big hug, then plants those magic lips on me again before walking out the front door, only wearing his underwear. When the door is closed, I take a deep breath and let it out slowly.

Seems Will's joke was on me.

HE HASN'T CALLED this morning. Not that I'm waiting for him to call. If last night was just a one-night stand, I'm perfectly okay with that. Not that I wouldn't love to ride that train again, so to speak, but it is what it is.

No regrets. That's my new motto.

In fact, it's probably for the best if it was just a one-time thing. I have baggage. And issues.

The doorbell rings, and I freeze. I'm *not* ready to see him. A phone call? Fine. But I'm not ready for him to be at my door. I'll probably do something silly and climb him again.

And if it's a process server, well, I'm not prepared for that either.

So, I do what any red-blooded woman would do. I hide in the closet.

My phone begins to ring, startling me. "Hello?" I whisper.

"Why are we whispering?" Jules asks, also with a whisper.

"Because I'm in the closet. Someone's at the door, and I don't want to answer it."

"Amelia Montgomery, you're a grown woman. If you don't want to answer the door, you just don't. You don't have to hide."

"I'm not hiding." I wince. "I'm totally hiding. I don't want to see Wyatt. I'm not ready for that yet."

"Who the hell is Wyatt?"

"My neighbor. The one who came over here in the middle of the night. And I totally had sex with him."

"What?" she screeches, just as the doorbell rings again. "Holy shit, Lia."

"I know, I fucked a stranger, and I feel a little slutty."

"As long as it was safe and consensual, why should you feel slutty?"

"It was those things. But I feel slutty because I barely know his name."

"Atta girl," Jules says with a smile in her voice. "But I still don't think you should be hiding in the closet."

My phone beeps with another call trying to get through. I check it and feel the butterflies in my stomach take flight. "He's calling through right now."

"Answer it!"

"I'll call you back."

"I'm staying on the line," she says. "Just switch over."

I grin and accept his call. "Hello?"

"Why aren't you answering your door?"

I bite my lip and consider lying, but then decide, *fuck it.* "Because I'm not sure that I'm ready to see you. I'm not trying to be a jerk, I'm just . . . dumb."

"Why?"

"Because, I don't know." I roll my eyes, sounding stupid to my own ears, and then remember Jules on the other line. "Hold on, I have another call."

I switch back to Jules. "It's him."

"And?"

"He's at the door and wants to know why I won't answer it."

"I'm wondering the same thing, honey." She laughs. "Go answer the door, and then call me later to give me the scoop. Oh, and I was calling to tell you that we're doing girls' night out Friday night. So don't make any plans with Sexy Neighbor."

She hangs up, and I switch back to Wyatt. "You there?"

"Yes. Open the door."

"What if I say no?"

"I'll go home. I won't like it, but I'll go home."

I open the closet door and peer out as if someone's going to jump out and murder me. Which is dumb. It's Wyatt at the door, not the process server or a serial killer. So I end the call and walk to the door, turn the knob, and pull it open slowly, expecting him to not look nearly as delicious as he did last night. It was just the heat of the moment. The lighting. The lack of sleep.

And when I see him leaning one shoulder on the doorjamb, his sunglasses propped on his head, his hazel eyes smiling down at me, I know I was right.

He's not nearly as delicious as he was last night.

He's much, much better.

four

Amelia

"Hi." I bite my lip and silently scowl at myself. Is that the best I can come up with? God, I'm so out of practice with this sort of thing. But then he smiles, that slow, Cheshire cat smile, and I forget all about how stupid I sound.

"You look fantastic this morning," he says, making me grin.

"You're sweet, but I don't. Not yet."

His eyes travel up and down my body, then land on my face again. "You look good from here. Grab your purse, I'm taking you out."

"Come again?" I feel silly standing in my doorway.

"Oh, you will," he says with a cocky smirk, and my sore lady parts pulse as I bust out laughing. "I'll take you wherever you want to go. Unless you really are allergic to the sunshine."

"I love the sun. But I'm busy."

"Doing what?"

"Working." I sigh and stand back, ushering him inside the house. "I just need an hour, and then I'll be happy to come spend the day with you. You can watch if you want."

That might have been a stupid move. I don't mind when people watch me work, but maybe Wyatt has other things to do.

"Cool," he says simply. "Lead the way."

I climb the stairs to the guest room where my studio is set up.

"More cameras," he says. "I'm intrigued."

I just smile and point to a chair out of range of the camera. "You can sit there."

He complies, leans his elbows on his knees, and watches me intently.

I take a deep breath while I make sure that I have everything I need for the video, then hit record.

"Hey, Beauty Brigade, I'm Amelia Montgomery, coming at you with a new makeup tutorial. I've had a slight change of plans for today. I know I told you all on my Instagram yesterday that I'd be doing a video about getting glammed up for date night, but my plans changed unexpectedly. Today, I'm going to walk you through my makeup routine when I don't have much time to get ready.

"In fact, this whole routine usually takes me about ten minutes if I'm not going through it step by step. So, let's get started, shall we?"

I glance over at Wyatt, who seems to be transfixed. "I'll edit this part," I inform him, and reach for my face primer.

"Okay, first—" I spend the next thirty minutes working through a simple makeup routine. It takes me longer than normal because I get tongue-tied a couple of times and have to go back, knowing that I'll edit the video later.

When my makeup is finished, and I've reminded viewers to subscribe to my page, I stop the recording, back it up a bit so I can listen to the sound, and then save everything so I can come back later for editing.

"Okay," Wyatt begins as I stand. "That was amazing, and I need to know more."

I grin, ridiculously excited that he's intrigued and not put off by what he just saw. "I'll be happy to answer all of your questions. But let's talk in the car. I could use some sunshine."

"My pleasure." He gestures for me to go ahead of him, opens the door to both the house and the car for me, and then sets off toward downtown. "So, you must be a YouTube vlogger."

"I am," I reply with a nod.

"How many subscribers do you have?"

"The last time I checked, I was just under three and a half million." I look over at him, curious how he'll respond to that. Vinnie used to *hate* it.

His gaze whips over to mine in surprise before returning to the road. "Wow."

"I mostly do makeup tutorials like the one you saw today. But I also do some fashion stuff, especially on social media. I have a makeup brand launching in a few months."

"Seriously?"

I nod happily, always excited to talk about this labor of love. And the fact that he hasn't said the words *stupid* or *ridiculous* are huge bonus points for him. "We'll start with an eyeshadow palette and four lip glosses, then build from there. I've already formulated everything, the colors are set to go, and I approve the packaging later this month."

"That's fantastic," he says. "And explains all of the boxes of makeup sitting on your dining table."

"Yeah, I get deliveries all the time. With my following, I'm considered an influencer, so companies send me products to use in my videos, to give reviews, that sort of thing. Sometimes, I'm sent to different locations for product launches and fashion shows. And I do some modeling for my own stuff, as well."

"You're busy," he says and reaches over to take my hand. I don't pull away.

I don't want to pull away.

"It's been a wild ride," I agree. "But let's be honest, I get to play with girly girl things every single day. It's the best thing ever."

He smiles. "You're a natural in front of the camera, and you're stunning."

"Thank you." I feel the blush on my cheeks, uncomfortable with the compliment, and glance out of the window, then point at a bakery called Succulent Sweets to my right. "Oh, stop here!"

"The bakery?" he asks, pulling into a parking space out front.

"Yes, I know the owner, and I need to send Will a thank you for the condoms."

I hop out of Wyatt's Lexus and hurry into Nic's bakery, happy to see her standing behind the case of beautiful sweets.

"Lia," she says with a smile and walks around to give me a hug. "I heard you were in town."

"Here I am," I say with a nod and then gesture to Wyatt. "Nic, this is my neighbor, Wyatt."

"I've already heard about you, too," Nic says, holding out her hand for his, and I scowl. Nic laughs. "Honey, news travels quickly in this family."

"You're related?" Wyatt asks.

"I'm married to Matt, Lia's cousin," Nic explains. "What can I do for you?"

"I need to send some thank you cupcakes to Will. Whatever his favorite is."

"So, every cupcake in the shop, because Will doesn't discriminate when it comes to food." She rolls her eyes as she reaches for a to-go box.

"Yeah, just throw in one of each," I reply with a nod, then pull out my phone to text Will. *Where are you? I have something for you.*

He replies almost immediately. *Just leaving training. Want to meet me here?*

Perfect! Yes, give me twenty.

I turn to Wyatt. "Do you mind if we run these over to him? He's just leaving training camp, and he's going to wait for us in the parking lot."

"Are you talking about Will *Montgomery*?" he asks and swallows hard.

"Yes, he's my cousin. Do you mind if we deliver these to him?"

Wyatt shakes his head. "I don't mind."

"He'll love them," Nic says as she passes the box to me.

"How much do I owe you?"

"Nothing. Family doesn't pay," she replies and waves me off.

"You're going to go broke," I say and pass the box to Wyatt when he reaches for it. "Our family is too big to always give out freebies."

"I think I'll be fine," she says with a laugh. "And I'm excited for girls' night out on Friday. I'll see you then."

"Absolutely. Have a great week."

We climb back into Wyatt's car. "Do you need directions to the training center?"

"Yes," he says with a laugh. "I don't exactly hang out there on a regular basis."

"It's easy, even I can remember how to get there, and I haven't been there in years." I get us off in the direction of where we'll meet up with Will and then look over at Wyatt and grin. "Are you overwhelmed by me yet?"

"I was overwhelmed by you last night," he says and pulls my hand up to his lips. "I'm more intrigued today. Do you know everyone in Seattle?"

"I'm related to almost everyone," I reply with a shrug. "We have a big family. I have two siblings, but I have six cousins, including Will. Seven if you count Natalie."

"Natalie?"

"Long story, but you'll probably meet her eventually." I feel my eyes widen and I cover my mouth with my hand. "I'm sorry, I'm being very presumptuous."

"Presume away," he says. "Keep talking."

"It's just a big, loud family. All of the cousins are married with kids, and we've brought their families into the fold. It's just a lot."

"And what are we thanking Will for?"

I grin. "He threw the box of condoms in my bag last night when I was at his place for dinner. He thought he was just being funny, but . . . here we are."

"I should have paid for the cupcakes," Wyatt says, making me laugh. I point to the little Mustang sitting in the parking lot ahead.

"That's him."

Wyatt pulls up next to him, and I get out as Will does, reach for the cupcakes in the back seat, and join him.

"Hey, what's up?"

"I brought you some grateful cupcakes."

"For what?"

I smile and glance over at Wyatt, who has just joined us. "For the condoms."

Will's eyebrows both climb onto his forehead, and then he pins Wyatt with a cold stare.

"Who the hell are you?"

"This is Wyatt," I reply and roll my eyes.

"Pleasure," Wyatt says, holding out his hand to shake Will's. Will's jaw is clenched tight, and he grips Wyatt's hand harder than necessary, making me roll my eyes again.

"Why are you trying to look like a badass? You're not Caleb or Matt."

He looks offended. "Caleb and Matt aren't the only ones who are badass."

"Well, stop it. I brought you food, and Wyatt's a nice guy." I prop my hands on my hips. "If you didn't want me to have sex, you shouldn't have given me the condoms."

"Give me the fucking cupcakes," he growls and then pins Wyatt with another grouchy scowl. "If you hurt her, I'll turn you inside out."

"So noted," Wyatt says with a nod.

"Good Lord, you're a caveman. I'm hungry, so we're leaving now." I pat Will's arm. "Go eat your empty calories. And save some for Meg."

"Meg didn't buy the rubbers," he grumbles as he climbs into his car.

"I'm starving," I say and then laugh. "And I'm sorry for that. Clearly, we're not dating or anything. I should have explained that to him so he'd lay off."

"I think if you'd have said, '*this is Wyatt, the guy I screwed in the middle of the night, but he's just my neighbor,*' I would be turned inside out right now. Besides, this is a date. So we're dating."

"Huh." I sit back as he pulls out of the parking lot, wondering how I feel about this.

Turns out, I don't feel half bad about it.

"Where should we go eat?" he asks.

"Do you mind if we head back toward our neighborhood and hit up Salty's? Unless you don't like seafood."

"Sounds great to me."

We're quiet as we make our way back to Alki Beach, soaking in the sunshine and comfortable silence. He's easy to be with.

Why did I find him annoying to begin with?

"SO, TELL ME more about you," Wyatt says after we're settled at the restaurant, an iced tea sitting in front of each of us, and two salmon Caesar salads on their way.

"No way," I reply, shaking my head. "You know a ton about me, and I don't know anything about you."

"What do you want to know?"

"Are you an only child?"

"No, I have two brothers, both older than me."

"Are they married?" I ask, sipping my tea.

"Nope, both single."

"Have *you* ever been married?"

"I am divorced," he says, nodding. "How about you?"

"The same." I sigh and squish the lemon in my tea with my straw. "I'm sorry, divorce is tough."

"Yeah, well, it's better than living with a cheater," he says and sips his own tea. His lips are sexy wrapped around that straw.

Am I seriously thinking about how sexy he is while we discuss something serious?

"It's also better than living with a jerk," I add, and we both nod. "What do you do for a living?"

"I'm an architect," he says, his hazel eyes lighting up.

"You love your job."

"I do," he says. "You get to play with girly things all day, and I get to build stuff. It's pretty cool."

"Did you love Legos when you were young?"

"I still love Legos," he says with a laugh. "Legos are my jam."

"Have you designed any buildings that I would know?"

"I don't work with a lot of commercial buildings. I mostly do private homes."

"That's cool. Big ones?"

He nods. "Yeah, the one I'm currently working on is a ten-thousand-square-foot home that will be built on the seaside."

"Wow. So, big and expensive."

"That's right. But this particular client is a challenge."

"How so?"

"She wants to change things every other day. By the time we get it the way she wants it, I'll be retired."

"She just knows what she wants."

"That's just it," he replies, frustration in his voice, "I don't think she *does* know what she wants, and that's why she changes it constantly. I mean, I'm paid hourly, so it's no big deal to me, except I have other projects to get to, and this one is taking up a lot of my time."

"I see. Well, it'll work out."

"Are you always this optimistic?"

"I guess." I shrug a shoulder. "I'm pretty blunt."

"I noticed," he says and squeezes my hand. "And I'm thankful."

"Last night wasn't typical for me," I inform him. "Seriously, I don't jump on random strangers."

"Good to know."

"In fact, I hadn't had sex in a long time."

"How long?"

"A long time."

His lips twitch. "Come on, that's subjective. It could be a week, or it could be ten years."

"More than a week, but less than ten years."

"You're stubborn."

"How long had it been for you? And if you say hours, I will leave you right now."

He laughs now, rubbing his hand over his face, and making me laugh, too.

"More than a year," he says. "I don't know the exact date, but it's been a while. My brothers were just ribbing me about it the other night."

"So maybe we were just scratching an itch."

His eyes sober, watching me as the waitress arrives and sets our food in front of us.

"Do you need anything else?" she asks.

Wyatt's eyes don't leave mine as he replies. "No, thanks."

She walks away, and neither of us moves. "I don't think I was just scratching an itch," Wyatt says.

"No?"

He shakes his head slowly, and huge butterflies take flight in my stomach. If I didn't know better, I'd say I was giddy.

"Okay."

"What about you?"

"I'm not sure." I tilt my head to the side as if I'm thinking it over. "Maybe we should scratch again, to see if there *is* an itch or if it's just chemistry."

"I like your smart mouth."

I lift my fork and dig into my salad. "That's good because it isn't going anywhere. And it might end up wrapped around you later."

He chokes on his tea, and I smile smugly while I chew my lettuce, waiting for him to recover.

"You okay?"

"You're going to be the death of me." He wipes his mouth with his napkin.

"Quite possibly." I nod and take another bite of salad, enjoying his company and the banter.

"How long have you lived in Seattle?" Wyatt asks, clearly changing the subject.

"I technically don't," I reply with a frown. "I grew up here, but I've been living in L.A. for about five years."

"So why are you living here now?"

"Well, there's some last strings to tie up with my ex, and my lawyer thought it would be good for me to have a change of scenery. Plus, I haven't been home in a long while, so it made sense."

"Your divorce is fresh then?"

"Technically, yes, but we've been separated for several years, so the end of the relationship isn't fresh at all."

He nods. "Did he cheat?"

"No, actually. And, before you ask, I didn't either. He didn't like what I did for a living. He said it was stupid, that the people who followed me were ridiculous because I don't have anything to offer them."

"So, he's a dick."

"Big time," I reply. "I think he was jealous that I was getting attention, and he definitely didn't like that I was beginning to make a living off of the way I look. Which sounds ridiculous."

"No, I get what you mean."

"But, I love it. And he couldn't support it. It turned verbally abusive, and finally, one day, I said *enough*. I'm out. And I never looked back."

"Am I a jerk if I say thank God?"

"No." I laugh and take another bite of my salad. "I say that all the time. And, frankly, I'm pretty happy that your ex was a cheater. Because I wouldn't be sitting here with you otherwise, and I've laughed more today than I have in a long time."

"Me, too," he says, setting his plate aside and reaching for my hand again. "Do you have plans for the rest of the day?"

"I do need to edit the video and upload it, so just a little work. But other than that, I'm free until girls' night out on Friday."

A slow smile spreads across his handsome face. "Perfect. How about I drop you at home so you can work, and I'll go do the same for a bit, and then I'll cook you dinner?"

"You cook?" I stare at him, shocked. "Like, more than macaroni and cheese?"

"Well, I won't make that now," he replies, making me laugh again. "Yes, I cook. I'm a single guy. If I don't cook, I starve."

"Or go out to eat all the time," I reply, already looking forward to seeing him later. "What time should I come over?"

"Six? Or whenever you're done with work. You can earn your keep and look beautiful in my kitchen."

"It's a tough job, but someone has to do it."

He pays the bill, and leads me out to his car, then drives me home.

"You could have parked in your own driveway," I say as I step out of his vehicle.

"I'm taking you home from a date," he reminds me. "And if you walked home from my driveway, I couldn't do this."

He pins me against the front door and leans down, one hand on my hip, the other caging me in. His lips graze over my cheek on their way to my mouth, and then I'm plunged into the sexiest after-date kiss on record.

My hands push under his shirt to his warm, smooth skin and hold on tight as his mouth plunders mine.

"You're so fucking sweet," he murmurs against me. "Come right over when you're finished working."

It's not a question. I nod and reach behind me for the doorknob, and sigh when I remember it's locked. I turn away from him to quickly unlock it, but of course, I can't get the key in the stupid hole, and I feel like a bumbling idiot.

Wyatt takes the little piece of metal from my fingers and helps me.

"Okay." I swallow hard. "I'll see you soon."

I step inside, close the door, and lean against it, willing my breathing to slow down.

Wyatt is one sexy man.

five

Wyatt

I've looked at the same email four times in a row, and I couldn't tell you what it says if my life depended on it.

I can't get a certain sexy blonde out of my head. Not only is she beautiful, but she's smart and funny. Honest.

Honesty is imperative.

I lived with a liar for more years than I should have. I won't do it again.

No, Amelia is a breath of fresh air.

I shut the laptop and walk into the kitchen. I haven't shopped in a few days, but there should be something here that I can whip together.

Just when I'm staring at the salad stuff, not impressed because we had a salad for lunch, the doorbell rings.

It's four thirty.

"Hey," Amelia says when I open the door. "I know I'm early, but you said—"

Before she can finish the statement, I pull her into my arms and kiss the fuck out of her, leaving us both breathless.

"You were saying?"

"I have no idea," she says with a laugh. I take her hand and lead her into the kitchen, where she sits on a stool and sets her phone on the countertop.

"Did you get your work done?" I ask.

"Yes, the video is uploaded; I'm just waiting for it to go live, so I'll keep an eye on my phone for a minute. I also went through and replied to comments on last week's video, then replied to people on social media."

"That's a lot of people interaction."

"Totally. But it's fun. I'd say ninety percent of the people who engage with me are nice."

"And the other ten percent?"

"Oh, they're creepers, mean girls, trolls. I skip over those. They used to really hurt my feelings or make me mad, but now I don't give them any energy."

"There's the optimism again."

She grins, her beautiful face lighting up. Her eyes are crazy blue. Brighter than the sky.

"I can't be depressed every day because people I don't know don't like me."

"Well, no. You can't." I lean on the counter and watch her, enjoying having her in my house.

"So, what are you making for dinner?" she asks.

I smile. "I'm not sure. My supplies are lower than I thought, so I'll probably just order from Uber Eats, if that works."

"You mean, I don't get to try out your stellar cooking skills?"

"Next time."

"Fine by me," she says with a shrug and then checks her phone. "Oh, there it is. I'm going to watch the first couple of minutes to make sure it's okay."

She presses play, and her voice comes out of the phone. Amelia is scrutinizing the screen, listening intently. After a short few minutes, she stops it and nods. "Not bad."

"I think it's pretty awesome."

"Thanks." She gets lost in tapping on her phone and scrolling, and then she finally turns off the phone and tosses it into her bag. "There. I'm not working any more this evening."

"Me neither."

"Did you get some work done, too?" she asks and props her chin in her hand.

"A little." I lean across from her, my arms folded over my chest. "Should we look through our options on the app?"

"I'm still fine from lunch," she says. "Do you mind if we wait a bit?"

"Nope." I push away from the counter and saunter over to her. She turns in her seat, fully facing me, looking up at me with happy, blue eyes.

My cock's been hard for her all damn day.

"How's it going?" she asks with a grin.

"I'm having a good day," I reply, cupping her face in my hands. I lean in to rest my lips against hers before brushing them back and forth lightly. "You?"

"Same," she says. Her hands make their way under my shirt, her fingertips brushing against the skin just above the waistband of my jeans. "I'm just the right height right now."

"For what?"

She pulls the button free on my jeans and pushes my T-shirt up my torso so she can lean in and press her lips to my stomach.

"Fun things," she says. "But I need you to take this off for me."

Only an idiot would ask why. I reach over my head and pull off the shirt, tossing it aside, and she gets back to work, kissing and touching me. She slips one finger under the waistband of my jeans and drags it back and forth, barely skimming the top of my cock with each pass.

"You're long," she comments, the words making me harder. "I like it."

"Glad to oblige," I reply with a laugh and then suck my breath in when she unzips my jeans and exposes me, then licks the head slowly. "Fucking hell, Amelia."

"I don't usually like it when people call me by my whole name," she says, casually checking out my dick. "But it's sexy when you say it."

With that, she takes the whole tip into her mouth and makes a pulsing motion with her cheeks, making my damn eyes cross.

Is there a volcano erupting right now? Or is that just me?

"Jesus." I push my fingers through her hair and grip her head. Not to try and guide her movements, but to have something to hold onto. "That feels amazing."

She hums against me and sinks lower, pulling more of me inside her mouth. She's shimmied my jeans over my hips, exposing more of me, and her small, magical hands are taking an exploratory journey over my skin that might make me come far faster than I'd like to.

"If you keep touching me like that . . . *God, Lia.*"

She smiles and keeps going, touching me, licking me. Finally, she sinks as far as she can and swallows around me, milking my cock.

How did I never get the blowjob of my life until I was in my thirties?

She begins to jack me off, and I can't take it anymore.

"I'm going to come, Amelia. If you don't want me to—"

But she shakes her head, holding and sucking harder, and I explode into her mouth, crying out her name.

When she's finished licking me clean, I pick her up, set her on the countertop, and rip her pretty pink panties in two, tossing them aside.

"You have a thing for ripping my clothes," she mutters but smiles as she pushes her fingers into my hair. "And I didn't bring the condoms."

"Don't need one," I reply breathlessly as I spread her wide and lean in to press my mouth to her center. I glide my hand up her stomach, over the thin sundress she's wearing, between her breasts, and urge her back onto her elbows. She props her feet on my shoulders, opening herself to me.

I sit back and take her in. It's not dark this time, and I can clearly see every delectable inch of her.

"So pink," I murmur, pushing my finger through her wet lips. "Responsive." She's clean-shaven. I can see her begin to swell, wanting me to fill her.

But not yet.

"Holy shit," she mutters, clenching her eyes closed.

"Watch."

She shakes her head back and forth, so I stop, and she frowns down at me.

"I said watch."

I push two fingers inside of her and press my thumb to her clit, and she tenses up. "Look at the way your muscles contract."

"Too much," she mutters, but I don't stop. "Want you in me."

"No way. I'm going to make your legs shake, baby."

She chuckles as if she doesn't believe me, but when I press my lips to her clit again, pushing my fingers against her inner walls, her legs do begin to spasm.

"What the hell?" she cries out as she comes around my fingers, against my mouth. "Holy fuck."

She's lying completely against the countertop now, her back arched, as the orgasm travels through her, and fucking hell if she isn't a joy to watch as she falls apart.

"My God," she mutters, catching her breath. "I didn't know that was possible."

I smirk and kiss her inner thighs, then up her stomach before helping her to a sitting position. She wraps her arms around my neck and pulls me in for a sweet hug.

"Are you okay?" I murmur against her cheek, then kiss just below her ear.

"Totally okay. I just can't move yet." She snuggles against me, holding on tightly as her breathing slows further, and our bodies calm. "I'm super hungry."

"We can find some food on the app," I reply, kissing her head and then pulling away.

"Okay." She kisses my chin. "But first, how about a tour of this beautiful house?"

"I thought you'd never ask."

I take her hand in mine and lead her upstairs first, to show her the bedrooms and the killer view.

"Wow," she breathes as she steps out onto the balcony off my bedroom. "This view."

"It's what sold me on the house," I reply and join her at the railing, watching sailboats pass on the Sound. "You must have a similar view."

"I do, but it always takes my breath away." She's leaning on the railing, the wind blowing the hair back from her face, and she seems perfectly content here. "If this was mine, I'd live out here."

"I use it quite a bit. My backyard faces the same way, but the view is better up here."

She smiles up at me, and I can't help myself. I cup her face in my hand and kiss her softly, just soaking her in. "Should we keep going?"

"Sure."

I lead her back through my room, show her the bathroom, and when I move to walk down the hallway, she doesn't follow.

"What's up?"

"This bathtub is insane," she says, running her fingertip along the rim of the tub.

"You'll have to take a dip in it sometime."

"Hell, yes," she whispers and then turns to take in the rest of the room. "There's lots of storage in here."

"I had this whole room remodeled before I moved it. It hadn't been updated in about twenty years."

"Well, you did a good job." She smiles as she follows me down the hallway, and I show her the guest rooms, then take her back downstairs to my office near the front door.

"No wonder you noticed me when I moved in. Your office faces my place."

I lean on the doorjamb and watch her saunter around my space, casually touching my pencils, my chair, looking at the books on the shelves.

She's damn sexy in my office.

"You went to Harvard?"

I smile and nod, enjoying her.

"Fancy," she says with a smile. Her blue eyes are bright and happy as she makes her way back over to me. "I like your space. It's bright and cheerful, but still masculine."

"Thank you."

She wraps her arms around my stomach and hugs me, resting her cheek on my chest. When was the last time I felt this comfortable with a woman?

Years.

I glance up and frown at the sight of someone pulling into her driveway. "Hey, look."

She turns around and frowns, then her whole body tightens up.

"Crap. It's my mom." She props her hands on her hips. "And my sister."

She looks up at me with apologetic eyes. "I think I'd better go see them."

"Let's go."

She frowns. "You definitely don't need to come with me."

"Unless you don't want me to, yes, I do. I'm having dinner with you, remember?"

She bites her lower lip, which only makes my dick twitch, and then shrugs one shoulder. "Okay, follow me."

I follow her across the street and am surprised at the family dynamic that unfolds in front of me.

"Hey, Mom," Amelia says, resignation ringing in her voice as she folds the older woman in for a hug.

"There you are," the older version of Amelia says. "You've been in town for *days,* and I haven't seen you."

"I know, I'm sorry, it's been busy."

"Too busy to call?"

Amelia glances over at me and gestures my way. "This is Wyatt. He's my neighbor, and he's been nice enough to befriend me. Wyatt, this is my mom, Sherri, and my sister, Anastasia."

Sherri's face immediately breaks out into a wide grin, and she holds her hand out for mine.

"Well, hello, Wyatt," Sherri says.

"It's a pleasure to meet you," I reply, and then turn to Anastasia, who seems a bit more reserved. She's beautiful, like her sister, but more simple. No makeup, casual clothes. "Hi, Anastasia."

"Hello," she says with a short smile. "How long have you known my sister?"

"A few days," I reply.

"So, you've made time for a stranger, but not for your family," Anastasia says, and Amelia immediately shuts down. Watching the shutters slam shut is fascinating.

"We can talk about this later," Amelia says. "Wyatt, maybe we should take a rain check on dinner."

"Not at all," I reply. "Why don't we all have dinner together?"

"Oh, I don't think—" Amelia begins, but her mom interrupts.

"That would be lovely, Wyatt. Thank you. Is that your house?"

"Yes, ma'am."

And just like that, Sherri is in the lead, guiding us back to my house, with the rest of us in tow.

"I'm famished," Sherri says. "What were you planning for dinner?"

"We were just going to have takeout," Amelia replies. "Wyatt, do you mind if we sit outside?"

"Not at all. I have a nice, covered patio this way."

Once everyone is settled with a cold drink, we decide on pizza from a place in town I haven't tried before and then settle in to talk.

Amelia is wound up tight, and if I'm not mistaken, nervous.

I don't sit directly beside her, even though I'm dying to touch her again. But I don't want to complicate things further with her and her family.

So, I hang back, playing the part of her friend.

"Have you always lived in Seattle, Wyatt?"

"Most of my life, yes. My family is here. I went away for college and then moved back to work. I'm an architect."

"How nice. Being near family is so important," Sherri replies. "Anastasia has just moved home, and Archer, my son, lives nearby. Now, if I could just talk Amelia into moving back permanently, I'd be a happy woman."

"Oh, Mom," Amelia says with a sigh.

"You've recently moved back?" I ask Anastasia, taking the focus off of Amelia.

"Yes, I've opened a wedding cake business over in Bellevue," she says with a nod. "I just signed my first contract today, in fact, so I'm officially in business."

"That's so great," Amelia says, a big smile on her face. "Way to go."

"Thanks. I tried to call you, but your phone was off, so Mom and I decided to just come over and surprise you."

"Especially since you didn't seem to be in a hurry to see *us*," Sherri adds, making Amelia scowl again. "I spoke to Jules the other day when I saw her at Gail and Steven's house, and she told me you were here."

"Mom, I'm sorry. It's been a busy week. I was planning to call you tomorrow."

"I was anxious to see you," Sherri says with a smile.

Man, parents sure can lay on the guilt trip.

I wonder if they offer a class for that when you're going through birthing classes because my mom is also the queen of the guilt trip.

"So, tell me more about the wedding cake business," I say to Anastasia, earning a scowl from Amelia. What did I do wrong?

six

Amelia

Why am I always attracted to men who flirt with anything in a skirt?

I blow my nose for the sixteenth time in about five minutes and hang my head in my hands. I feel like my face is going to explode.

And I'm moody as fuck.

Perfect time for my phone to ring.

"Heddo."

"Lia?" It's Jules. "Are you okay?"

"Caught a cold," I reply and wipe my already red and swollen nose. "God knows where."

"I'm sorry. Do you need juice? Soup? NyQuil?"

"I've already ordered all of that. Should be delivered sood."

"Well, you sound miserable, honey. I hope you feel better for girls' night on Friday."

"I will," I promise her. "What's up?"

"Well, *your* mom called *my* mom, who called me. And your mom likes Wyatt."

"I'm sure." I blow my nose again and then feel my stomach sink, the same way it did yesterday when we were over at Wyatt's house. "But I'm not so sure that I like Wyatt right now."

"Why?"

"Vinnie was a fucking flirt, Jules. He would flirt with *anyone.* But he had a habit of flirting the most with Anastasia."

"I remember. The slimeball flirted with *me*, and I thought Nate was going to take his testicles off. But what does that have to do with Wyatt?"

"Well, Wyatt insisted that we have dinner with Mom and Stasia, which didn't thrill me. I mean, he's not my boyfriend, and he's new. I wasn't exactly ready to introduce him to my family. But it happened, so whatever. But when we were all together, he kept flirting with Stasia. Asking her all about her job and paying way more attention to her than I was comfortable with."

"Well, she was new to him, so maybe he was just making small talk?"

"Maybe, but it felt way too similar to Vinnie, and anything that reminds me of him turns me off."

"As it should," she assures me. "Is it worth having a conversation with Wyatt to tell him that? Or will you just move on?"

"Right now, all I want is a fucking nap," I reply. "So, I think when the delivery arrives, I'll take some NyQuil and sleep the rest of the day away. Then I'll think about Wyatt and why all men feel the need to be charming."

She chuckles in my ear. "That's probably a good idea."

"Hey, were you calling for anything specific?"

"Not really. I was going to suggest lunch since I'll be out your way later today, but we can do it another time. Get some rest, and don't worry about the man across the street."

"Thanks, girl." I hang up and blow my nose, just as there's a knock on the door. It's my grocery delivery, thank God.

But I don't even have the opportunity to take the cold medicine before my phone pings with a text.

From Wyatt.

Please come help me. I think I'm dying.

I frown, still irritated with him. But I like him well enough to not ignore a cry for help. So, I load my sickness supplies back into their bag and walk across the street.

"Heddo?" I call out as I walk through the front door. "Wyatt?"

"In here," he replies from the living room. I walk in and stop cold, taking in the scene before me. Wyatt's lying on the couch, one arm flung over his face. There's a pile of used tissues on the coffee table, and a box of clean ones on his belly.

"Hi," I say simply. He moves his arm and peeks at me.

"Are you here to save me?"

"From what?"

"Death."

I smirk, walk to him, and press the back of my hand against his forehead. His nose is red, but his cheeks are pale. "No fever. You're not dying."

"I feel like I'm dying," he says and sits up, then immediately reaches for another tissue to blow his nose. I snag one for myself. "Did you catch this?"

"Have you seen me?" I ask and then raise my eyebrows when he looks up at me. "Clearly, I did. I don't usually sport the red nose."

"You look beautiful," he murmurs, then sneezes into his tissue. "Can you please make me some soup? Do you *have* soup?"

"Actually, I did bring my soup over to share," I reply and walk into his kitchen. "It's just out of a can."

"Perfect," he says. "Thanks. Are you okay?"

"I don't feel great," I reply. I'm not in the mood to discuss dinner last night. I'd be happy to never have to discuss it again. "But I'll be okay."

"Well, you're doing better than me because I'm not entirely convinced of my survival right now."

"God save me from the man cold," I mutter as the soup heats up on the stove.

"Is it cold in here?"

"A bit," I reply and walk over to fetch a blanket that's folded on the back of a chair, then drape it over him. "Here, this will help."

"Thanks." He pulls the blanket up under his chin, and I roll my eyes as I walk over to dish up the soup for both of us.

"Soup's on," I announce as I carefully carry a bowl to him, setting it on the coffee table.

"No crackers?"

"I don't use crackers, sorry," I reply. *If you want crackers, buy your own fucking crackers.*

But I don't say it because he doesn't feel well, and neither do I, so I'm probably just overly touchy today. Dramatic. On edge.

Just as I sit to eat my own soup, he scowls.

"This is too hot."

And, we're done here.

"You know what, fuck this." I set my bowl down and stand, reaching for my grocery bag. I open the NyQuil and take half the pills out, setting them on his counter. "I'm sick too, Wyatt. And I can *not* deal with your man cold today. So here's some medicine, you have your soup, and you can just deal with the rest of it on your own. I don't particularly want to hang out with you after yesterday anyway."

"What do you mean—?"

"No. I'm out of here. I need a nap, my own bed, and I need to be alone. Goodbye."

I march out of his house and over to mine. My phone is ringing in my hand, with Wyatt's name flashing, so I decline the call and put my phone in airplane mode.

I want everyone to leave me the hell alone.

Once I've taken my medicine and crawled into bed, sleep comes swift and hard.

I SLEPT FOR six hours. It was marvelous. My head is still packed, and I think I might resemble Medusa with the flying hair and crazy face, but at least I got some sleep.

I turn my phone on and sigh at the nine texts and two calls from Wyatt, not to mention the six hundred notifications on social media.

Six. Hundred.

I need an assistant.

I don't check any of it. Instead, I set my phone aside and pad into the kitchen for some orange juice. I left my soup at Wyatt's, so I don't have any of that, but I do have crescent rolls in the fridge. I'll just bake those up and eat them all.

Carbs don't count when you're sick.

I do thumb through some of the social media messages while the rolls bake. Some are from trolls, and those get deleted immediately. I answer a few of the easy questions and then set my phone aside again when the rolls are done.

I didn't realize how hungry I was. Just as I set them all on a plate with a side of marinara, my doorbell rings.

If it's Wyatt, he can just turn around and go home.

I open the door, only wide enough for my eye to peep through, and scowl.

"Hello, Wyatt."

"I'm here to apologize for being a prick," he says and holds up some beautiful flowers. "Please, let me in."

I open the door and walk to the kitchen. I hear him walking behind me.

"I brought you soup, from Lily's."

"Lily's, the deli?" I ask, my interest piqued.

"Yes, ma'am. I also brought ice cream."

Okay, maybe he can hang out with me for a while. "What kind?"

"Cookies and cream."

I turn to look at him. His nose is still red, and his eyes are tired. But they're also full of hope and apology, and that's what gets me.

"The flowers are pretty."

"Also for you," he says with a half-smile. What is it with men and their half-smiles that get a girl every time? "I truly am sorry. I was a complete baby, and that's not okay. Ever, but especially when you're also sick."

"It's not okay, *ever*, Wyatt. It's not sexy, and it's not fun. I was married to that for far too long, and I hated it." I bite my lip. "But I also overreacted, probably because I'm also not feeling well, and I'm sorry for being short with you."

"I understand," he says with a nod. "I can promise to be an adult when I'm sick in the future."

I take the flowers and put them in water, quiet while I work. "I don't know if this should continue," I finally say and turn to face him.

"What do you mean?"

"Seeing each other." I bite my lip as he frowns. "Not just because of today. I mean, the man cold is annoying, but if it was a deal-breaker, relationships wouldn't last through flu season."

"So why then?"

"You're nice. The sex is fun. I like being around you when you're healthy."

"Yes, I can see why we should stay far away from each other."

I laugh and push my hands through my hair, reminded that I need a shower. "Okay, I'm going to be real with you because I don't feel great, and I don't have the brain space to dick around."

"Excellent. Always be real with me, Amelia."

I seriously love the way he says my name.

"I didn't like the way you were talking to my sister yesterday."

He frowns. "How was I talking to her?"

I sigh, realizing that this sounds absolutely ridiculous. Crazy, even. "Okay, backstory. My ex flirted with *everyone*. My family included. Especially my family, probably because he knew it drove me nuts."

"I wasn't flirting with your sister," he says, frowning.

"You took a lot of interest in her," I reply. "And please understand, I don't think you were hitting on my sister not even thirty minutes after you'd been intimate with me. I don't think you're a monster."

"Well, that's encouraging." His eyes are narrowed now, and he looks genuinely pissed off. "I was engaging your sister in small talk to take your family's focus off of *you*, Amelia. They were both hell-bent on making you feel like shit for not calling them the minute you got to town, and I could see how uncomfortable you were."

"Oh."

I hadn't considered that.

And I feel ashamed. Deflated. And honestly pissed because, again, I let my past relationship influence my reactions to a man who has been nothing but wonderful to me.

"I don't know your family dynamic, and it's honestly none of my business, but it frustrated me, and I was trying to help, not piss you off."

"I wasn't pissed." It's a total lie.

"Yes, you were. Otherwise, you wouldn't be talking about not seeing me again."

I shrug. "Okay, I was pissed."

He walks to me and folds me in his arms, holding me close. He presses his lips to my forehead.

This is unexpected. I tell him I can't see him anymore, and he holds me?

"I have baggage," I murmur into his chest. "I guess I didn't realize how much."

"We all have baggage," he replies and nudges my face up to look at him. "But don't run from me, Amelia. Talk to me. Let me help, or apologize, or work on it. Don't run."

"This is still new, Wyatt."

"And it's the best thing that's happened to me in a long time. I'm not afraid to admit that." He kisses my forehead again. "Now I know what one of your triggers is, and I can make sure you aren't uncomfortable in the future. You just have to tell me, baby."

"Are you for real?" I stare up at him, completely surprised by him. "You're not a robot, are you?" I pinch him.

"Ouch." He rubs his arm. "A robot wouldn't have been a whiny baby over having a cold."

"Ah, yes. You're real. I'm sorry for the way I acted. Truly."

"Apology accepted."

I stand on my tiptoes to kiss his chin, then turn to the soup he brought. "I'll share my soup with you, but not my crescent rolls."

"Greedy," he says with a smile, watching me. "Let me stay tonight."

"There will be no sex tonight, Wyatt." I can't help but laugh. "I'm way too sick."

He drags his hand down my back. "No, but there can be cuddles and Netflix."

"Netflix and cuddle sounds better than Netflix and chill," I say with a happy sigh. "Okay, I'm in."

"OH MY GOD, this is so good," Samantha Nash says after the first bite of a lemon cupcake. "Seriously, Nic, they just get better and better."

"The recipe doesn't change," Nic replies with a laugh.

"I can't get enough of them," Sam shrugs.

We're at Succulent Sweets, Nic's bakery, for girls' night out. Jules and Natalie are arranging fruit, nuts, cheese, and meats on a board. There is a pink cocktail being poured, and gorgeous women surrounding me.

I hope I remember everyone's names. I *do* remember whom each of them is married to, so I silently go around the room, committing faces and names to memory.

Nic is married to Matt. Sam is Luke's sister and is married to Leo freaking Nash. As in the lead singer of Nash. As in one of the most famous rock stars in the world.

I met him at Will's wedding and almost made an absolute fool of myself.

Alecia, the curvy blonde laughing with Sam, is married to Dominic, and that's a whole crazy family story. But I love both of them. Dom is calm and broody, and so smart, and Alecia is his perfect match.

Of course, Meg is here, drinking her pink cocktail and talking with Meredith, who is married to Sam and Luke's brother, Mark.

This is so fucking confusing. I need a roadmap.

"Where are Stacy and Brynna?" Nat asks.

"They both have sick kids at home," Jules says. "Speaking of which, how are you feeling, Lia?"

"So much better." I accept the pink cocktail and take a sip, then feel my eyes go wide. "Oh, this is good."

"Be careful, you'll get hammered fast," Sam says with a wink. Sam is also blond and super petite. She has a runner's body. "So, tell me why we're at the bakery instead of one of the fun bars downtown for girls' night."

"Because," Meredith says, "we're too old to go clubbing. This way, we can drink and eat and talk without the crowds."

"It's quieter," Alecia adds.

"We're old women," Sam mutters but reaches for another cupcake. "But I guess if I can have leftover cupcakes and cocktails all night, it's not so bad."

"Not to mention," I add with a smile, "we don't have to close down at two. We can party all night if we want to."

"I don't remember the last time I partied all night," Jules says with a smirk. "I'm so domesticated."

"Why didn't Anastasia come?" Natalie asks.

"She's finishing up a wedding cake for tomorrow. One of the tiers fell today and spattered all over the floor, so she has to remake it."

"Oh my God, that's a baker's worst nightmare," Nic says, shaking her head in sympathy. "Please remind her that if she ever needs help, I'm happy to lend a hand."

"I will, thanks."

"Okay, we're all set up," Jules announces with a wide smile on her beautiful face. "We have food over here, so we all don't go into a sugar coma."

"I'm happy in my sugar coma," Sam says, raising her cupcake in salute.

"We also have cocktails and wine for *days*," Natalie says, laughing at Sam.

"Hallelujah," Alecia says.

"And I brought something, too," I add, all eyes immediately pinned on me. I turn and reach for the huge tote I brought in with me and lift it onto a table. "You guys know that I always have deliveries from makeup, hair care, and skincare companies. I use some of it, but not all of it is good for my coloring or skin type. Or I just have so much of it, I could never use it all."

"You brought us goodies!" Meredith exclaims.

"I did. All of this is for you. Please don't make me take anything but the tote home."

"We get to shop," Nic says with a smile, and leans in to hug me. "Thank you."

"This party is for *you*," Nat says. "You weren't supposed to bring us stuff."

"But thank you," Meg adds. "Because since Erin was born, my skin has been so dry."

"Oh, I have stuff for that."

We spend the next hour eating cake, food, and drinking pink cocktails while I give makeup tips. It's the most fun I've had in *years*.

"Amelia has a boyfriend," Jules announces, much to my horror.

"No, I don't."

"Well, you're fucking him, honey, so unless he was a one-night stand . . ."

"He could be her fuck buddy," Meredith suggests.

"Is he your fuck buddy?" Alecia asks as she rubs a makeup remover wipe over her forehead.

"I don't think—"

"Oh, you have to talk about it," Meg interrupts with a Cheshire cat smile. "It's part of girls' night out. We talk about sex. It's what we do."

"It is?"

"Fuck, yes," Nic says. "Except Jules gets grossed out because we're fucking her brothers."

"Will and I don't fuck," Meg reminds everyone. "Don't let him hear you say that."

I can only laugh and watch these gorgeous women banter with each other as they play, elbows-deep, in my makeup and skincare leftovers. Sam has frosting on her cheek. Meredith does a pirouette on her way to the cocktail station.

"So, spill it," Meredith says. "Tell us everything."

"Don't forget to use the dirty words," Sam adds with a sage nod.

"Well, he's my neighbor," I begin and see Nat frown. "He's the guy in the white house kitty-corner to yours."

"Oh, he's handsome," she says with a smile. "I haven't met him, but I've seen him outside now and again, and he's not bad to look at."

"I'll have Matt do a run on him," Nic says as she picks up her phone. "What's his last name?"

"What do you mean?" I demand.

"To make sure he's not a pervert or a murderer or something," she says with a shrug.

"Crawford. His last name is Crawford."

"On it," Nic says, biting her lip as she texts her husband. "Keep talking."

"He's an architect. And he introduced himself the day I moved in."

"Nice," Alecia says with a nod. "That means he's friendly."

"Or casing the joint," Nic adds.

"You've been married to a cop for way too long," Nat says, making Nic smile.

"Anyway," I continue. "I ended up needing his help in the middle of the night, and then I climbed him like a tree because he was standing in my kitchen in nothing but underwear."

"As one does," Sam says with a nod.

"And now I can't shake him." I shrug and reach for a cupcake.

"That's it?" Meredith says with a frown. "You didn't use *any* dirty words."

"I mean, we've fucked a few times. And he makes my legs shake, which has *never* happened to me before."

"Now it's getting good," Meg says, rubbing her hands together.

"Isn't the leg shaking thing the best?" Jules asks.

"I had no idea," I reply. "And his tattoos? Holy shit."

"Where are his tats?" Nic asks as her phone chirps. "Matt says he checks out clean."

"That's a relief. He has a full sleeve," I reply. "And I want to bite every inch of it."

"Is he pierced?" Jules asks with a sly smile.

"Like, his ears?"

They all look at each other and then bust up laughing. "Not exactly," Jules replies.

"I'm missing something."

"Is his dick pierced?" Meg asks.

"No." I scowl and then feel my eyes go wide. "Whose dick is pierced?"

"Nate's," Jules says and then takes a satisfied sip of her drink. "And let me tell you, it's *ridiculous.*"

"I don't think I've ever known anyone with pierced genitalia."

"Well, now you know two," Meg says.

"Will's pierced, too?" I screech, making them laugh.

"No, I am," Meg says. "Orgasms galore, my friend."

"Reaaaaally." I tap my chin, thinking about it, and then quickly decide that no one is coming near my girl places with a needle.

"How are *your* orgasms?" Sam asks.

"So good," I say. "I mean, shaking legs aside, the rest of it is stellar. The man knows his way around a woman's body."

"It's always a bonus when they don't need Siri to direct them to your G-spot," Sam says with a nod.

"I have to ask you a question," I say to Sam, who just lifts an eyebrow. "What's it like to have sex with a rock star?"

A slow smile moves over her lips. "Oh, honey, it's everything you'd expect and more."

"Wow." I swallow hard. "Are you going to kick my ass if I admit to you that I have a crush on your husband?"

"Not today," she says as she reaches for another cupcake. "Because most of the world does, and I just don't have the energy to beat up most of the female population."

"We all have some pretty fantastic men," Alecia says with a satisfied sigh. "Like, *really* fantastic."

"We're a lucky bunch of bitches," Meredith adds.

"With some *amazing* orgasms," Meg reminds us, just as her husband walks through the door.

"You'd better be talking about me, Lazy Bones."

"Oops, I've been caught," she says with a laugh. "Why are you here? This is girls' night. And where is your daughter?"

"With my mom. When are you coming home? It's late."

"After we're done playing with makeup and drinking pink drinks and talking about sex. Lia's having some good sex these days."

"I don't want to know," Will says, pinning me with a scowl.

"Your fault," I remind him. "You supplied the condoms."

"I'm too damn giving."

seven

Amelia

I'm just pushing my feet into four-inch Jimmy Choos when Wyatt rings the doorbell a week later. He's taking me out to dinner tonight with his brothers, and I want to make a good first impression.

I do a quick study in the mirror. Little black dress that shows a touch of cleavage, check. Makeup and hair looking pretty fantastic, even if I do say so myself, check.

Fuck-me heels, check.

I grin, reach for my clutch, and walk to the door, opening it wide and smiling at an incredibly sexy Wyatt. He's in slacks, a green button-down shirt with the sleeves rolled high enough for his tattoos to peek out at me, and his usually tousled hair is tamed back.

I can't wait to sink my fingers into it later.

"Hi."

He frowns and takes me in from head to toe.

"You can't go out like that."

I glance down at myself and then scowl at him. "What do you mean?"

"My brothers will hit on you, and then I'll have to fucking kill them."

I smirk and walk past him, closing the door behind me. "Well, I'm not changing, so you'll just have to control yourself."

He mutters something about assholes under his breath, making me giggle, and then opens the door for me. Before I can sit, he leans in and presses a kiss against my neck, just below my ear.

"You're stunning." I smile up at him. These words mean the world to me, to have him notice that I put in the extra effort to look nice for him.

"Thank you."

The sun is just setting into the Sound as we drive around Alki Beach, headed to downtown Seattle.

"Where are we going tonight?" I ask.

"There's a place downtown called Palomino. Have you been?"

"I've heard of it," I reply. "I've heard good things."

"I like showing you new things," he says and kisses my hand, making me soften just a bit. He says sweet things. All week, he's been attentive, kind, and just a little bossy in the bedroom.

Okay, a lot bossy, and I have to admit, it's sexy as all get out.

He parks, and we walk the block or so to the restaurant. It's a Friday night, and the city is busy, the air is warm, and there's an energy sparking between us tonight that hasn't been there before.

I can't put my finger on what it is, but it's thrilling. Sexy.

Intimate.

He holds the door for me and tells the maître d' who we're here to see. We're led through the bustling restaurant to a table with two ridiculously handsome men already seated.

They both stand when they see us and greet me with wide smiles.

"You must be Amelia," the first one says. "I'm Levi."

"Jace," the other says, shaking my hand. "And you're beautiful."

Wyatt growls, literally growls next to me, making me laugh. He pulls out my chair for me, and I sit, already charmed by his brothers.

"Which one of you is the oldest?"

"Me," Levi says.

"And what do you do for a living, Levi?" It's not lost on me that this is very similar to the conversation that Wyatt had with my sister the other night and, suddenly, regret fills me again for how I reacted to it. He was taking an interest in my family, and I'm grateful.

"I'm a detective for the Seattle PD."

I feel my eyes widen. "Wow, thank you for your service. How long have you been doing that?"

"About fifteen years," he says with a shrug and sets his menu aside.

"That's a long time. You must enjoy it."

"I take pride in what we do," he replies thoughtfully. "There are days I love it, and others that I hate it."

"I understand," I reply softly. "What do you do, Jace?"

"I'm a doctor," he says with a smile. "And you?"

"Oh, no. It's still your turn. What kind of doctor?"

"I'm a surgeon," he replies, and my eyes immediately fall to his hands. His fingers are long, manicured. Smooth. Steady.

"Did you all go to Harvard?" I'm smiling at all three now, enjoying their company.

"No, I went to the police academy," Levi says, shaking his head. "These two are the Ivy Leaguers in the family."

"I went to Duke," Jace replies.

"You're all so fancy," I say and wink at Wyatt, who hasn't taken his hand off my knee since we got here.

"What do you do, Amelia?" Jace asks and brushes his hand on my arm. Just in a friendly way, but I feel Wyatt's grip on my knee tighten so I cover his hand with mine and give it a squeeze, reassuring him that I'm here with *him*, and I'm just getting to know his family.

"Please, call me Lia. I'm actually a beauty blogger. I have a channel on YouTube where I give tutorials on makeup and skincare, and I'll be launching my own makeup brand soon."

Levi's eyes narrow. He probably thinks that this means that I'm basically unemployed, which is what most people think. They have no idea that this can be a lucrative career.

"She's amazing in front of the camera," Wyatt adds and smiles down at me. "She's articulate, knows the products she's talking about, and looks amazing."

"Thank you," I reply and lean in to kiss his shoulder. His support means more to me than he could possibly know.

"Interesting," Jace says, nodding. He looks over my shoulder and frowns. "Cruella, six o'clock."

"Fuck," Wyatt mutters, just as a woman sidles up beside him and offers all three men a fake smile.

"Funny meeting you guys here," she says, then looks at me. That fake smile falls right off her face when she sees Wyatt's hand on my leg. "Hello, I'm Claudia Crawford."

Ah, the ex-wife.

I would be lying if I said I haven't been dying of curiosity to know what she looks like.

She's on the short side, with blond highlights in muddy brown hair. Her makeup is caked on, only enhancing the wrinkles around her eyes.

I could teach her so much.

She looks older than I assume she is, but her eyes are shrewd, and not happy.

"Hello, Claudia," Wyatt says with a sigh.

"You must be the flavor of the month," she says to me, and Wyatt's eyes narrow menacingly.

"This is Amelia, my girlfriend."

My whole body stills at this comment. *Girlfriend.*

Am I his girlfriend? It makes me glow rather than want to run away. This is something I need to think about later.

But Claudia's eyes turn glacial now.

"I see."

Wyatt stands, dwarfing Claudia. "Is there something you need?"

"I just wanted to say hello to you all. I haven't seen you in a long time, and you know I always liked your brothers."

"Can't say we liked you back," Jace replies, leaning back in his chair. *Awkward.*

Her eyes narrow, and without a word, she glares at all of us and then quickly stomps away.

Wyatt sits again and blows out a long breath.

"I'm sorry about that."

"I don't think you have anything to be sorry for," I reply. "Is her name Claudia or Cruella?"

Levi grins. "To her face? Claudia. But we've called her Cruella for years."

"We're not fans," Jace says, winking at me.

"So I gathered."

"You dodged a bullet there, brother," Levi says and sips his wine. "A big, nasty bullet."

Jace laughs and touches my arm again.

"If you want to keep your million-dollar hands, you'll stop touching her."

I cock an eyebrow, and Jace just laughs again but raises his glass in a toast. "So that's how it is."

"That's how it is," Wyatt confirms.

"I wasn't hitting on you," Jace says. "He just seems to be touchy."

"This is new," Levi adds thoughtfully. "Interesting."

"Really?" I look at Wyatt, who just sips his wine and doesn't change his facial expression. "Do you want me to change the subject?"

"That would be fantastic," he replies.

"Have you heard from crazy house lady lately?"

"I LIKE THEM," I say as I walk into my house and flip on the light. "You're all very different, but it's *so* interesting to see how similar your body language is."

I kick off my shoes and set my clutch on a table and turn in time to see Wyatt making a beeline for me, lifting me in his arms and pinning me against the living room wall, kissing me silly.

Well, hello there.

I dig my fingers into his over-long hair and hold on tightly. He's in a fast mood tonight, and I never know how or where he's going to take me when he's like this.

It's thrilling.

"You're so fucking sexy," he growls against my neck. I'm suddenly on my feet, and he's turned me around and is kissing the back of my neck. His hands cup my breasts, teasing the nipples into hard points with his fingertips. "Your body comes alive when I touch it."

"You're good at touching it," I reply, already panting and throbbing for him. But he gathers my dress in his hands and begins to pull it up over my ass, so I quickly turn to face him, not wanting him to see my backside.

I have ass issues.

I cup his package through his pants, and he goes right to work kissing me, his hands moving all over my body.

Finally, he takes my hand and guides me up to the bedroom. He flips the sidelight on, and we fall onto the bed, all tangled arms and legs and lips.

He turns me over, but I squirm under him and switch onto my back, shaking my head.

"Turn the light off."

He scowls. "I want to see you."

"Okay." I push up to kiss him, but he makes a move to flip me again, and I shake my head. "I want to see you, too."

His eyes narrow, but he doesn't argue. He just gathers my dress in his hands again and tugs it over my head, throwing it over his shoulder.

"Fucking Jesus, if I'd known *this* was what was under that dress, we never would have left the house."

I grin. I'm in black, lacy underwear that shows off all of my curves. So rather than ripping it all in two the way he normally does, Wyatt takes his time, kissing every inch of flesh as he uncovers my skin, setting me on fire.

"You're good with your mouth," I whisper, reveling in the way he lingers, licking me with just the very tip of his tongue, sending electrical currents humming through me.

"I can't get enough," he says, surprise heavy in the words. "No matter how much I get, it's never enough."

I'm tugging at his clothes, frustrated that he keeps moving out of my reach. "You need to get naked, babe."

He kisses my palm, then sits up to discard his shirt. My hands immediately find his chest, gliding down to his flat, muscled stomach.

But it's always the tattoos that catch my eye.

"I love your ink," I whisper.

"I know," he says and covers me again, kissing me as if it's the last time. He grips my wrists and pins my hands over my head, making my back arch, giving him better access to kiss and taunt my nipples.

My legs are restless, squeezing to find some relief from the pressure building, but Wyatt grins and maneuvers between them, spreading me wide.

"Wyatt."

"Yes, baby."

"I'm gonna need you to—" I gasp when he drags two fingers down my torso, over my pubis, and through my slick folds.

"What?"

"I don't remember."

He chuckles. "Say it."

"I need you." I hear the whimper in my voice but don't have enough wits about me to care. "Inside me."

"In here?" he asks, pushing his fingers into me, stretching me deliciously.

"Oh, yeah."

"Does that feel good, beautiful?" He plucks my nipple with his lips, making a smacking sound as he fucks me with his fingers, still pinning my wrists with his other hand. I feel the tension building.

"Jesus, I'm going to come."

"I certainly hope so." He presses his thumb to my clit, and it's all I need to fall over the edge.

He kisses me deeply, still fondling me lightly, and when my body calms, he reaches for the box of condoms, suits up, and guides himself inside me.

But rather than taking me fast and hard, which I'm expecting, he takes long, slow strokes as if his dick is memorizing every inch of my pussy.

He brushes the pad of his thumb over my lower lip, watching me intently.

I squeeze and watch in satisfaction when his eyes close, and he loses control, coming around me and in me.

He buries his face in my neck, breathing hard, still shivering.

"Incredible," he whispers before he moves off of me, and shifts to my side, pulling me to him.

I let my eyes close, just intending to rest, but fall into sleep, listening to Wyatt's heartbeat against my ear.

SOMEONE IS DOING marvelous things to my back.

I'm coming out of sleep and realize that I'm on my stomach. Naked.

I'm on my stomach naked.

I fling my eyes open and look over my shoulder at Wyatt, who's braced over me, kissing my shoulders.

And my ass is naked.

With the lights *on.*

I move to turn over, but he calmly holds me in place and continues his kissing spree.

"I think these shoulders are so damn sexy." His tongue travels from one side to the other. "Firm, but feminine. And the way the muscles curve in to your spine is hot."

"I have a bony back," I reply, still tense. Vinnie used to tell me all the time that for a skinny girl, I sure had the fattest ass out there. I've mastered the art of camouflage with clothes. I make sure I have sex on my back, or in the dark.

And now I don't have any of that armor on me, and I might have the first panic attack of my life.

"Wyatt—"

"Shh. Did you know that you have two perfect little dimples right over your ass?"

Fuck. Yes, and cellulite for days, if the truth be known.

"You're safe here," he says quietly, and tears immediately spring to my eyes. He kisses just above my ass crack, then sinks his teeth into the fleshy part of my left cheek. I bite my lip, suddenly incredibly turned on, but still self-conscious.

"Wyatt, I appreciate you wanting to make me feel—"

"Sexy? Desired? Hotter than fuck? Because that's what you are. I can tell that you have issues with this part of your body." His hands slowly move up and down over my cheeks, massaging firmly. "I don't know why, and I probably don't *want* to know why. But I can tell you this. I've never seen a woman that I want more in all of my life, Amelia. Your ass is heart-shaped, and the perfect size for my hands."

I grip my pillow when his fingertips move inside my upper thighs, gently brushing over my swollen lips. Dear God, every time he does this, I'm convinced that I've never been more turned on in my life.

This is no exception.

But this time, I'm not just turned on, I'm self-conscious and trying really hard to let go of that.

It's not easy.

"And it leads to the most amazing pussy," he whispers, pressing a wet kiss to where my ass meets my thigh. He braces his forehead on my butt and sighs deeply. "I want to sink inside you so badly right now, but we used the last condom earlier."

"Oh, I've been on the pill for years," I assure him, needing to feel him inside me again. "I can't get pregnant."

"Amelia."

I turn to look at him and see so much in his eyes. Affection. Lust. Trust.

It's the trust that makes my heart stutter because by God, I trust him, too.

"You can trust me," he says.

"I know." I bite my lip, take a deep breath, and brace on my knees, pushing my ass in the air.

"Jesus," he mutters before sliding inside me, making us both sigh in pleasure. "I just . . . fuck, Amelia."

"So damn good," I agree with a smile.

eight

Wyatt

I didn't plan to fall in love again. No fucking way. Not that I planned to be celibate for the rest of my life either. That would just suck.

But amicable, physical relationships were all that appealed to me. Until Amelia.

I'm not saying I'm in love with her. I don't know that yet. But I do know that I'm taken with her. I want to be with her, and when I'm not, my mind wanders to her. She's been bad for my productivity at work.

But she's the best thing that has happened to me in a long, long time.

I'm on my side, my head propped in my hand, watching her sleep. The early morning sunshine is coming through the window, lighting up the room. Her lips are parted slightly as she dreams.

I swear to Jesus, I've never seen a more beautiful woman than Amelia in my life. Not just because she's physically stunning, but because of who she is.

Honest.

Funny as hell.

She loves her family.

And she's vulnerable while being incredibly strong. I've known that she has a hang-up about her ass. Flipping over every time I want to take her from behind isn't exactly hiding it. I'd like to deck the bastard that ever dared to make her feel less than amazing.

But, she's mine now. And I intend to make her feel safe every damn day.

She turns toward me and rests her hand on my hip, then buries her face in the pillow and goes back to sleep. I can see her phone behind her on the bedside table. It's on silent, but it keeps lighting up with notifications. It's been doing that all damn night.

The woman needs a break from work.

I kiss her forehead and ease out of bed, careful not to wake her. I pull on last night's clothes, then hurry across the street to my house and change.

Maybe we both need a break from work this weekend. Nothing crazy, but something to get us out of the house and away from our desks. I prop my hands on my waist, look blindly around the room, thinking. Then the sunlight on the Sound catches my eye, and an idea takes root.

I hurry to the closet and pack a bag for a couple of days. Then I hurry down and load it into my car, glancing over at Amelia's house. No movement yet.

I'd like to be the one to wake her this morning.

So I hurry down the street to a café and order us both coffees and pastries, and then rush into a small grocery store for waters and snacks.

I pull into her driveway and walk into her house, stopping to listen. No movement.

She's still in bed when I walk into her bedroom, on her belly now, hugging the pillow and snoozing away. I set our coffees on the table next to her and climb onto the bed.

"Amelia," I whisper into her ear. She wiggles her nose.

"Mm."

"Amelia," I repeat and kiss her cheek. "Wake up, sweetheart."

"No," she murmurs, making me grin. "Tired."

"I know, but I need you to wake up."

I brush her hair off of her neck and press a kiss there. "Come on, baby."

"No sex," she says and yawns. "You got enough last night."

I cock a brow. "No amount of sex is ever enough with you," I reply. "But no, I'm not trying to have sex with you right now."

One eye opens to a slit, and she observes me.

"You're dressed."

"Yes, ma'am."

"Why are you dressed?"

I chuckle and kiss her cheek again, "You just told me that you're not in the mood for any more sex."

"So?" She reaches out, and her hand finds my thigh. "You're in jeans."

"Nothing gets past you, does it?"

She frowns and boosts herself up onto her elbows, giving me just a peek of her breasts.

"Hey, caveman, I'm up here."

"You have a crease right here from the sheet." My finger follows the line across the top of her breasts, and her breath catches.

"Have I mentioned that I sincerely like your hands?" she asks. "They do nice things to me."

I just shake my head and watch her as the sleep leaves her eyes.

"I smell coffee."

"Took a minute."

"Don't make me hurt you. I just woke up."

"Violent, aren't we?"

"If you don't give me the coffee, you'll see violence."

I laugh and reach for our cups and pass her one.

"You went to the café? What time is it?"

"It's only eight."

She sits up, tucks the sheet around her, and frowns at me. "You're awfully perky in the morning. Is this normal? Because if it is, it could be a deal-breaker."

"Would you rather I was grouchy?"

"I'd rather you were asleep." She takes a sip and then tips her head back and moans, making my dick twitch. "But this is lovely. And you're very sweet to me. I'm sorry I'm so grouchy in the morning."

"I need you to get up and pack a bag," I inform her before I strip naked and pound her into the mattress until neither of us can feel our legs. "The sooner, the better."

"Why?"

"Because I'm taking you somewhere, just for the weekend. Nowhere fancy. In fact, think *very* casual. Just the basics."

She tips her head, studying me with her hands wrapped around her hot cup. "Casual and basic." She thinks about it as she takes another sip of her coffee. "Okay. Do you have to go pack?"

"I'm ready to go when you are." I climb off the bed and smile down at her. "And I'm anxious to get on the road."

"Where are we going?"

"Don't worry, you won't need your passport."

"YOU KNOW," SHE says two hours later as we sit on the ferry and watch Seattle disappear into the water behind us. "I've never been on a ferry."

"Really?"

"Nope. It's kind of fun."

I drape my arm over her shoulders, and she leans into me, resting her head against me. I bury my lips in her hair and take a deep breath, taking in the smell of her.

"How often have you been to the San Juans?" she asks. I had to tell her where we were going once we got to the ferry. Her face lit up with excitement.

"A few times," I reply. "I've never been where we're staying, though. It has great reviews, and it's close to the beach as well as other things like hiking if you're interested."

"I even brought appropriate shoes," she says with a chuckle. "And I'm warning you, I brought very little makeup. Mostly just skincare stuff. You said we were taking the weekend off, and for me, that means little makeup."

"Excellent." I kiss her head again. "You're gorgeous with or without the makeup."

"And you're charming," she murmurs. "Can I ask some questions?"

"You can ask all of the questions, anytime you want to."

She pulls away so she can see my face. "Even if they're questions about your ex?"

"Sure." Being honest with her is always my intention, even if it makes me uncomfortable.

"I wouldn't normally ask, but after seeing her last night, I'm curious."

"I understand." I brush a piece of her hair off her cheek. "Go ahead."

She looks out at the water as if she's pulling her thoughts together.

"You've already told me what led to the divorce, so I don't have any questions about that. Infidelity is a deal-breaker, every time."

"Agreed."

"I guess it's interesting to me because your brothers do *not* like her. Did they like her before the divorce?"

"I think they liked her in the beginning." I also stare out at the water, thinking it over. "They were always kind to her because she was mine." I feel Amelia tense up next to me and I glance her way. "Are you sure you want to talk about this?"

"Of course."

"I think she was different back then. She looked horrible last night. She never used to try so damn hard to look young."

"It only makes her look older," Amelia's voice is soft.

"You're right. She *did* always have a bit of an attitude, and there were moments that her snarky side would come out, and I'd have to tell her to reel it in.

"But when we were married, and things were good, she never turned the snark on me. Does that make sense?"

She nods, waiting for me to continue.

"I never planned to divorce her. Not until the day I walked in to see her fucking the pool guy on the kitchen counter."

Amelia gasps and stares up at me in horror.

"Yeah, pretty clichéd, right?" The outrage doesn't come back like it used to when I think back on it. "Leading up to that day, we'd had a couple of rough years. I wanted kids, and she didn't."

"You didn't talk about that before you got married?"

"Oh, we did." I nod and then shrug. "But she claimed to change her mind. I felt the distance growing over time."

"But you were committed to staying."

"Of course. Marriage is serious to me, Amelia. I married her for better or worse, 'til death parted us. It's kind of a big deal."

"I agree, and I'm not saying that it's not a big deal. It's the biggest deal. But I think that a lot of people these days assume they'll get married, and then if it doesn't work out . . . *oh well*, we'll just get a divorce."

I nod. "You're right. Some do feel that way. I'm not one of them."

The ride on the ferry is smooth. The sun is shining, and sailboats glide by. We can see islands in the distance.

"Why do your brothers call her Cruella?" she asks with a smile.

"Because it's funny."

"It really is," she replies and chuckles. "Do you see her often?"

"No." I pull her back into my arms and hug her close. "I hadn't seen her since the day the divorce was final. Of course, I would run into her the day I was with you."

"Is it weird that I hate that she didn't change her name?" she asks quietly. "I mean, this is just fun between us, and I'm certainly not staking a claim or anything, but it's weird that she didn't change her name. I changed mine the second I could."

We're going to talk about this claim-staking nonsense later.

"I didn't ask her why she didn't change it," I reply. "Maybe it was for convenience."

"Maybe."

"Any more questions?"

"Not today." She smiles up at me, and I can't help but lean down to kiss her lips.

"Well, good, because we're almost there." I point off to the distance, where we can see an island coming into view. "And I refuse to talk about unhappy things on our short vacation."

"Agreed." She nods once. "And in case I forget to tell you later, I had a really good time."

I stand and tug her into my arms, hugging her and rocking her back and forth, completely at home with her wrapped around me.

"Me, too, sweetheart."

"SO, WHAT YOU'RE saying is, this is something you like to do often."

She's panting in front of me, hiking up the trail in the woods not far from our resort. The trees are bright green, and the whole place reminds me of a rainforest. It's damp; birds sing above.

It's perfect.

"Hiking is good for the soul."

"It makes a girl sweat," she says, but she's not whining. She's just matter-of-fact, and it makes me laugh.

"Well, yeah. You didn't seem to mind sweating last night."

"That's different." She looks back at me and sticks her tongue out, then marches ahead. "I have to admit, though, it's beautiful here. I live in a concrete jungle most of the time, and I forget that places like this exist."

"You're in good shape," I comment. "It doesn't seem like this is too hard for you."

"Of course, it's not too hard for me," she replies, shaking her head. She insisted on carrying her own pack full of supplies when I offered to take everything in mine. She hasn't complained a bit. "I can do it. I just don't usually choose to hike in the wilderness. I lean toward girly things. Like shopping."

"Nothing wrong with that."

"But I'm not just a girly girl," she continues loudly. "I'm also a badass."

"Never said otherwise. But I would like to know why you're talking so loud."

She turns and props her hands on her hips, frowning at me. "So the animals can hear us coming and run away without eating us."

"Exactly what kind of animals are you evading?" I can't help but smile, delighted with her.

"You know. Bears. Lions. The kind that eats people."

I step to her and drag my thumb over the apple of her cheek, enjoying her. She's sans makeup today, and I secretly think she's more beautiful this way, although I'll never say that to her.

"Amelia, there are no bears or lions on this island. We're not in Alaska. Or Africa, for that matter."

"Nothing can kill me here?"

"No."

She loosens up, her muscles letting go of the worry, and her whole face lights up. "Awesome. I'll still talk, though, because that's what I do."

"I hope so."

She turns and continues walking up the trail. "In fact, I think I'll see if Jules and Nat want to shop sometime this week. The fall lines are starting to show up in stores, and I want a peek at them."

"Have you enjoyed being home with your family?"

She nods. "Oh, yeah. I didn't know them well when I was a kid because I was *so* much younger. But now as adults, we get along great, and have a lot in common."

And how much longer are you here?

Rather than ask, I hurry to catch up with her and take her hand in mine, threading our fingers.

She's here today, and I'm enjoying the hell out of her.

"TODAY WAS PRETTY great," Amelia says. We're sitting on the balcony of our room, which looks out to the ocean. We can't see it now that it's dark, but we can still hear the waves crashing against the shoreline.

We just finished dinner, and Amelia is sitting back in her chair, one heel tucked against her ass so her knee is up against her chest, and she's sipping her wine.

"You even left your phone in the room."

She looks down at the device sitting on the table. "Yeah, and I turned off all of my notifications, aside from text messages. This is a vacation, right?"

"I'm impressed," I reply and reach over to tug her foot into my lap. I dig my thumb into her arch, and she sighs in happiness.

"You're good at this pampering thing."

"I just took you out of town and am rubbing your foot."

"Exactly," she says and takes a sip of wine. "You're rubbing my foot. Good things will come to you, my friend."

I frown down at her toes and then look up at her. I wasn't going to ask this weekend, but I need to know how much time I have with her.

"How long until you go back to L.A.?"

She pauses, takes another sip of wine, and then sets the glass aside. "I'm not sure."

"Are you saying you're in Seattle indefinitely?"

She frowns. "I honestly don't know how long I'll be here. I've planned on a couple of months at least."

She climbs out of her chair and into my lap, wrapping her arms around my neck and hugging me close.

"I know that I'm enjoying you while I'm here," she says. "And that sounds lame, but I really *am* enjoying you. And I will keep you posted when I know more."

"I would appreciate that."

Her small body fits perfectly against mine. She's gently running her fingers through my hair, making me sleepy.

"I like your hair," she says softly. "It's one of the first things I noticed about you. You wear it long."

"Would you prefer it short?"

She kisses my forehead. "I like it as it is. You don't need a cut yet."

Suddenly, her phone pings with a text. Without leaving my lap, she reaches over to snag it.

"It's Samantha," she says.

"Who's Samantha?"

"Natalie's sister-in-law," she informs me as she opens the text. Her whole face breaks out in a happy smile. "Oh, she's inviting us to go to a Nash concert next week."

"Us?"

"Yeah." She looks at me and bites her lip. "I might have talked about you during girls' night out last week?"

"Is that so?" I press a kiss to her shoulder. "What did you say?"

"That you're horrible." She giggles as she replies to Samantha. "And not fun in bed at all."

"So, the truth then."

She laughs harder now, and my cock comes to full attention. It seems that happens no matter what we're doing.

"Are you free on Wednesday evening?" she asks.

"Sure. How did she get Nash tickets? It's been sold out for months."

"Oh, she's Leo's wife."

I'm certain I've misheard her. "What?"

She sets the phone aside after replying and wraps her arms around my neck again. "Yeah, she and Leo are married. So we'll go to the concert, and then they're having a party at their house after. I guess it's the last show on his tour, so they're celebrating."

"You know Leo Nash."

She frowns. "Yeah."

"Luke Williams, the movie star, Will Montgomery, the football player, and Leo Nash, the rock star, are all part of your family."

She shrugs one shoulder. "I know, they're a lot. But, yeah, they're my family."

"You're an interesting woman, Amelia."

"Oh, you don't know the half of it. That side of my family is full of all kinds of fun stories. Do you want to hear some?"

"Will there be a quiz later?"

"Possibly." She laughs and then clears her throat. "Okay, Jules is the youngest sister. She married her boss, Nate, about five years ago. They started their own company, and they have a daughter."

"Pretty normal stuff."

She nods. "Natalie is Jules' best friend. Her parents died when she was young, and Jules and her family pretty much took Natalie in as part of the family. So I really consider her a cousin. She's the one married to Luke."

"Get to the good stuff."

"You're not a patient man." She reaches for her wine and takes a sip, emptying her glass, then reaches for mine. I just smirk and watch her sip my wine. "Will is next. You've met him. He's married to Meg, who's a nurse at Seattle Children's. Now, Meg and Leo Nash used to know each other when they were kids in foster care. Like, way back in the day. They even had a band together, but then Leo went to L.A. to pursue music, and Meg went to college to be a nurse.

"They didn't meet back up again until a few years later when Meg had already met Will. But Leo is like a brother to her. He met Sam through Meg, and it was love at first sight, or so the story goes. Actually, Sam was kind of a bitch to him, but he liked her."

"Is there a book that goes along with this so I can keep it all straight?"

She just laughs and tucks her hair behind her ear. "I know, I told you it's a lot. Let's see. You've met Nic, and she's married to Matt, who's a Seattle cop. Oh! I bet he knows your brother."

"I'm sure they probably know each other. You'll have to ask Levi the next time you see him."

She nods thoughtfully. "I will. Okay, Caleb is a former Navy SEAL. We don't even want to know some of the things he's seen. He's married to Brynna, and they have three kids. Brynna's cousin is Stacy, who is married to the oldest Montgomery brother, Isaac."

"Jesus, I hope there's no quiz," I mutter, making her laugh.

"Isaac and Stacy have two kids. And then we have Dominic, who none of us knew about until like four years ago."

"What do you mean?"

"Well, it seems my uncle Steven had a very brief affair early in their marriage. They already had a couple of kids, and they were separated. I don't know the whole story, but lo and behold, there's Dominic."

"How did that go over?"

"I was already living in L.A. when all of it went down, so all of this is hearsay, but it didn't go over well at first. But now, they're just one big happy family. Dom owns a winery just south of Seattle and is married to Alecia."

"Is that it?"

"I think so," she says with a laugh. "You're going to meet most of them next week, so I thought I'd give you a brief overview."

"That wasn't brief."

"You know what else isn't brief?" she asks as she slinks out of my lap and takes my hand, guiding me back inside.

"What's that?"

"What I'm about to do to you in the shower."

"Lead the way, sweetheart."

nine

Amelia

Vacations never last long enough. Especially the kind that is a surprise from a guy who you're quickly falling for.

How did this even happen? Is it too good to be true? I've been pondering this since we left Seattle two days ago. I've never met a man like Wyatt. Aside from the men in my family, I thought such men were urban legends because I'd never met one in real life that I wasn't related to.

And yet, here we are.

We're on the ferry, headed back to Seattle, and I'm not ready for our little bubble to burst. I don't even *want* to know what my notifications look like on social media. I didn't even load a video for the week yet, and that's absolutely not okay.

That's my livelihood.

So, that'll be the first thing I work on when I get home.

Wyatt went to find us bottles of water a few minutes ago, and I've just been enjoying the summer breeze on the water and watching the world float by us. It feels lazy. Indulgent.

Lovely.

My phone pings with a text from my attorney, Pam.

I'd like to chat with you tomorrow. What time works?

I scowl, feeling the bubble bursting already, and reply.

Morning is fine, just call when you're ready.

I glance up as Wyatt turns the corner and tuck my phone away. I'm not going to think about this anymore today. I gave Vinnie *years* of my life, and I'll be damned if he gets to interrupt one of the best weekends I've had in a long while.

No, I'll tuck that away and deal with it later.

"Sorry, there was a line," he says when he passes me the water.

I take a sip and then lean my head on his shoulder, tracing the ink on his arm. "How long have you had these?"

"I just finished it last year. I started it when I was in college."

"Wow, that's a long project."

"Well, I never intended for it to be a sleeve. It just evolved over time."

I nod.

"Are you okay?" he asks softly.

"Sure, why do you ask?"

"You're quiet."

"I don't want to go home yet." I chuckle. "I didn't mean for that to sound whiny. I don't remember the last time I took some time off from work, so this was a treat."

"I had a good time, too," he says and kisses the top of my head. "We can try to take more weekends off together."

"I think I'll be working long days this week making up for this weekend," I reply honestly. "I'll eventually need to hire an assistant."

"I know that time off only adds to your workload, but you need it, Amelia. You need to recharge."

"I know. This weekend reminded me of that. I didn't intentionally become a workaholic, you know. I buried myself in work when I was with my ex because work was my happy place. And then things just exploded, and if I don't work on it every day, I get so far behind that it's maddening. So, it's really a habit. Not to mention, when you work from home, it's easy to become a workaholic."

"I know," he replies, nodding. "I'm the same way, for some of the same reasons. But it's been . . . *good for me* to spend time with you. For many reasons."

I need to hug him. I've never been a big hugger, but it seems that all bets are off when it comes to Wyatt.

I wrap my arms around his middle, the way I've come to love to do. He's strong, and he wraps himself around me, making me feel safe and cared for.

Not that I need him to take care of me, let's make that clear right now. But I do need the hugs.

He rocks me slowly back and forth for a long while, with the wind blowing around us and the birds flying by. It almost feels like we're the only two people in the world.

"You're amazing," he whispers before pulling away far enough to tip my chin up with his finger and lower his mouth to mine.

This kiss is sweet. Slow. Thorough. He's always thorough when it comes to kissing me, his tongue and mouth exploring me as if he's never kissed me before.

And when he comes up for air, we're both panting.

"Stay with me tonight."

It's not a request.

"I'll just have to go home and get a few things," I reply. "And I *will* have to spend the day at home tomorrow."

"I understand." He leans his forehead against mine. "But I'm not ready for this to end. I want another night with you. Just you and me."

"I'm on board with that."

He sighs and brushes the hair from my cheek. He's always finding ways to touch me, whether it be in the throes of passion, or on a ferry in the middle of the Puget Sound.

And I am soaking it up like a sponge that's been left in the desert for a month.

"HI, PAM," I say the next morning. I've been home for an hour, and just got out of the shower and pulled on some shorts and a tank top. It's hot outside today. I think I'll work on the patio, next to the pool.

"How are things in Seattle?" she asks.

Too damn good.

"Fine, actually. How are things down there?"

"You haven't had anyone try to serve you papers?"

"No. Where I'm staying isn't in my name. It isn't even in my family's name. No one would think to look for me here."

"Excellent," she says, satisfaction in her voice. "So, the good news is *you* haven't been served papers. But the bad news is, neither has he."

"What? How is that possible?"

"He refuses them. Literally won't take them."

"He's such an ass." I sit and rub my fingers over my forehead. "Now what?"

"Oh, we'll get him served. Don't worry. It's just taking longer than we thought. So the way it looks right now, you'll be in Seattle for a while longer."

"That's fine, actually. I have a nice place, my family is nearby, and I'm working."

I'm also fucking my neighbor, and I think I've fallen in love.

But she doesn't need to know that.

"I'm glad you're comfortable. Let me know if you need anything, and I'll be in touch."

"Thanks, Pam."

I hang up and want to throw my phone across the room. Who the fuck does Vinnie think he is? And *why* is he doing this?

I would talk to him, just *ask* him, but frankly, I don't know what he would do. I don't trust him not to hurt me.

No, I'm safer here in Seattle, letting Pam handle everything.

Lord knows I'm paying her a pretty penny to take care of it.

The doorbell rings, and for a moment, I'm afraid again. Maybe it's a process server. Or Vinnie himself.

But that's just stupid.

I walk to the door and look outside. There are two men. One is a UPS driver with something for me to sign, and the other is my older brother, Archer.

I smile widely and open the door.

"Delivery, ma'am," Archer says with a sarcastic grin.

I sign for the package, then walk inside, gesturing for Archer to follow. As soon as I set the box down, I turn and launch myself at him, hugging him fiercely.

"You didn't even call to tell me you were coming over."

"Surprise," he says, then sets me down. "You don't look like shit."

"Did Mom say that I looked like shit?"

"She said you looked tired," he says, his Montgomery blue eyes suddenly serious. "And she said you're hiding something."

"Mom's always been a dramatic one," I reply, rolling my eyes and walking into the kitchen to pour us each something to drink. "Let's sit out by the pool. It's too nice outside."

"How did you score this place?" he asks, looking around. "Wait. This is familiar."

"It's Natalie's house," I reply as we walk outside and sit in the shade, next to the pool. "She's letting me use it while I'm in town."

"Much better than a hotel," he says with a nod. "So, what are you hiding?"

"Psh." I shake my head and drink my lemonade. Archer is the one person in this world that I *cannot* lie to. I've always been closest to him. I tell him all of my secrets. "Nothing."

"Liar." He sips his drink and then crosses his ankle over his knee, waiting patiently. My brother is a big man. Tall and broad, he looks like he could play ball with Will. But he's the gentlest man I know.

"So, remember when I got divorced, and you, Stasia, and the 'rents came to L.A. to throw me a small party in celebration?"

He nods, his eyes narrowing.

"And how I am about to sign with a cosmetics company for my makeup brand?"

"Of course."

"Yeah, so, it turns out that I'm *not* actually divorced."

He swallows, looks away, fisting his hands, and every muscle in his body tensing. If Vinnie were standing before him right now, he'd be unconscious.

"What the fuck did he do?"

"Contested."

I tell Archer all about Pam calling me into her office, coming here, *everything,* and it feels better than I thought it would.

"So, Jules and Nat know."

"Yeah."

He swallows and rubs his hand over his face.

"But *we* don't know."

"Archer, there was no way in hell that I was going to bring you all into this. Not after all of the shit you already went through because of Vinnie. It was *over.* It *is* over. This is just a technicality, and my attorney is handling it."

"You've been pushed out of your own home," he says, anger vibrating off of him. "Don't get me wrong, I love that you're home, but Jesus, Lia, this isn't something that you need to go through alone."

"I'm not."

"I'm so damn pissed at you for not telling me. You should have called me as soon as you got here."

"I'm not nine," I reply, angry myself. "I'm not a child, Archer. I'm handling this the best way I know how. I know you're all here if I need you, but this is really *just* a technicality. I'm divorced. I worked too damn hard to get where I am to let Vinnie fuck this up for me. I'm moving on with my life."

"Are you? Because you can't even launch your brand until this is wrapped up. Not to mention, you're *not* divorced."

"Stop it. I am. And this will be over soon, and I'll go back to L.A. and be out of your hair."

"Why?"

"Why what?"

"Why do you have to move back to L.A.?"

I stare at him. "Because it's where my work is. My condo. My car. My life."

"All of that is easy to move here. You don't have that asshole tying you down there anymore, Lia. You can just as easily live in Seattle."

"My makeup brand will be launching out of L.A."

"Commute for that."

I frown and look down. Honestly, I've been seriously considering this over the past week or so, but I'm not ready to talk about it. Not yet.

"I'll think about it."

"Good." He smiles at me. "Do you have any food?"

"What is it with you and Will and eating us all out of house and home?"

"I'm a growing boy," he says, rubbing his belly.

"Ew. I don't want to know."

"If you don't want to feed me, I could just throw you into the pool." I cock a brow. "Do *not* do that."

"It looks warm." He stands, and I run away from him, but he catches me, lifting me into the air.

"No! Archer, I'm serious, do *not* throw me in that pool. I just dried my hair, damn it!"

"You can dry it again."

"No. No no no no no."

I'm giggling until he walks closer to the edge.

"Damn it, Archer, no."

"She said no."

Archer stops, and our gazes fly to the man standing at the other end of the pool, near the entrance of the house. His hands are fisted, and his eyes are lethal.

Wyatt wants to deck someone.

"Wyatt, this is—"

"I don't give a fuck who he is. You'll take your hands off of her. Now."

"Or what?" Archer asks as he lowers me to the ground and walks around the pool toward Wyatt.

"For fuck's sake, stop it." I run to catch up with Archer and stand between him and Wyatt. "I said stop it."

"Who is this joker?" Archer asks. I plant my hand on his chest, then turn to see Wyatt glowering down at me and my hand currently touching my brother.

"This is Wyatt," I reply. "My neighbor from across the street, *and* my boyfriend. And Wyatt, this is Archer, *my brother.*"

"Yeah, I'm her brother," Archer says, narrowing his eyes.

"For the love of God, stop with the posturing. It's exhausting and ridiculous."

I walk away, leaving them to beat the hell out of each other if they want to. So be it. I'm not a fucking referee. What is it with men and their egos? My ex was the absolute *worst*. He drove me absolutely nuts with it, and I refuse to put up with it from these two.

I walk into the kitchen to pour another glass of lemonade. Archer comes in behind me.

"I'm going to go," he says, surprising me. "But I'll be back soon. Text me. If you're in town, I should see you more often."

"Uh, okay. What the hell just happened, and what did you do with my brother? Did you drown him?"

He grins. "Wyatt and I talked. We're cool." He waves as he walks out of the house.

I turn to put the pitcher in the fridge and hear the glass door shut behind me. I don't turn as I start to speak.

"You know, I don't appreciate—"

I don't have a chance to finish before he takes the glass out of my hand, sets it on the counter, and turns me around to look at him.

"You know what I don't appreciate, Amelia? I don't appreciate walking in here to find you in another man's arms. Laughing and squealing and having a good time while that man touches you."

"Jesus, he's my *brother*." *Don't do this.* Don't turn into a jerk now.

"I didn't know that," he says. He's breathing hard, his chest is heaving, and his hands keep curling in and out of fists by his sides. "All I knew was that he had his fucking hands on you."

"He's my brother," I repeat and push my nose up near his. "And you just walked in here like you own the place."

His eyes narrow.

"I can hang out with whomever I please. I don't have to ask your permission. I don't have to ask for anyone's permission for *anything*."

He cages me against the countertop, still not touching me.

"Do you think this is about me wanting a say in who you hang out with? Are you that blind?"

"I think you're acting ridiculous," I counter, frustration vibrating through me. "You went all caveman without just asking who he is. I wasn't having sex with him. We were playing around, Wyatt."

"Let me turn this around on you, sweetheart. If you walked into my house, and I was holding onto a beautiful woman, a stranger to you, how would that make you feel?"

I immediately see red, but I just clear my throat and school my features. "I would calmly ask if I was interrupting."

He leans in farther and plants his lips against my ear. "Bull. Shit."

"Now I'm a liar?"

He laughs and shakes his head, but there's no humor there.

"If you're this mad at me, you can just leave. No harm, no foul. Because I won't be told who I can have fun with, Wyatt. I've put up with that shit in the past, and I won't do it now, not even for you."

"I'm so damn frustrated," he growls. "I can't even touch you. I'm afraid of hurting you."

His jaw clenches, and a piece of his long hair falls onto his forehead. I can't resist reaching up to smooth it back, and the next thing I know, he's kissing me like a man possessed.

"I wanted to kill him," he mutters as he kisses his way down my neck. "I was going to rip his fucking arms off."

"Violent."

"Deserved," he replies. "You said the other day that you're not staking a claim; well I'm telling you right now, I *am*."

He picks me up and carries me into the living room, laying me on the couch the same way he did the first night we had sex here.

"Wyatt—"

"Stop talking." He's making quick work of sliding my clothes off, kissing my skin, making me come alive beneath him. "I've never been a jealous man, Amelia. I can put up with a lot. But seeing another man touching you seems to be my breaking point. If you're not ready to call this a relationship, so be it, but that's exactly what we're in, Amelia."

His fingers are doing delicious things to me, moving through the lips of my pussy, making me so damn wet and needy, I don't even know who I am right now.

He pushes inside me and stops when he's balls-deep.

"This? This is mine, Amelia, do you hear me?"

I can't look away from his intense hazel eyes. They're on fire as he watches me, making it clear in no uncertain terms that he's here to stay. It should terrify me, but it only makes me want him more.

"Say it."

"Yours."

"What's mine?" He's moving now, roughly, pushing me hard toward the finish line. "Tell me."

"My pussy is yours."

"No." He stops now and holds my face in his palm. "*You*. All of you is mine."

My heart shatters as his eyes fill with tears, and I know that I've fallen just as hard as he has. I *am* his.

And he's absofuckinglutely mine.

"I'm yours, Wyatt."

"That's right," he says, tipping his forehead against mine as he thrusts in and out of me, sending us both into the stratosphere.

"But, Wyatt?"

"Yes, baby."

"You're mine, too. This isn't one-way."

"No. It isn't one-way."

ten

Amelia

"Seeaaaaattlllle!" Leo screams out into the crowd, making the whole place erupt into absolute, adoring chaos. "I fucking love you!"

Wyatt is holding my hand, and he gives me a squeeze. I glance up and smile at him happily. My cousins have been giving him the side-eye all evening, and I'm sure there will be some interrogations later, but Wyatt's been completely calm, having a great time.

"Look, there's Meg!" Jules yells, pointing as Meg walks confidently out on stage, holding a guitar. She's gorgeous in a short, black dress that flows around her legs, and her hair is wild with pink streaks running through it.

"I fucking love it when Meg sings," Nat says, clapping excitedly.

The whole Montgomery clan is crammed into the first two rows, just in front of the stage to the right side so we can see everything perfectly. Leo knows how to end a world tour.

"This is Meg," Leo says, gesturing toward her with a grin. "Y'all remember her, right?"

Key Arena explodes into applause again, making Meg grin from ear to ear.

"We're going to sing a couple of songs together," Leo says, then takes the mic away from his mouth and leans in to say something to Meg. She nods and begins to play the guitar. "This is one we used to sing all the time, back in the day when Meg was in my band."

She walks up to her mic. "You mean when you were in *my* band."

She winks at the crowd, making them laugh, and Leo just shakes his head.

Leo Nash is sexy as fuck. I glance over at Jules, who just winks at me. He's the consummate rock star: tattooed and pierced, his hair messy, gauges in his ears. I never would have paired him with Samantha, but she's gazing up at him from a few chairs away from me with lust and so much love, I'm surprised she hasn't exploded with it.

They break out into an old Coldplay song, and I begin to dance around. Wyatt has moved throughout the night, but suddenly, he starts dancing. And I don't just mean stepping back and forth.

My man can *move*.

"Damn, you're good at this," I say, and he winks down at me, sweeps me into his arms, and moves us in the sexiest circle that's ever existed.

If we weren't surrounded by about a billion people, I'd climb him right here and now.

When the song is over, Wyatt dips me deeply and then pulls me back up to kiss me silly.

My cousins applaud.

"What's next?" Meg asks Leo. Without a word, he breaks out into another song, and she easily keeps up.

"I love P!nk," Stacy says. For the next thirty minutes, Meg and Leo rock the stage, until finally, Meg pulls her guitar off and takes a bow.

"She's damn good," Wyatt says.

"She really is," I agree. Meg joins us as Nash breaks out into more songs from their extensive backlist, rocking for another thirty minutes.

"Jesus, how long are they going to play?" Brynna asks. "They have to be exhausted!"

"It's the last night, so they'll play for a while," Sam says, watching her husband. "And Seattle is their favorite crowd."

"I can see why," Nat replies. "Are you sure you want all of us to come over tonight? Don't you want him all to yourself?"

"I'll have him," she says.

"Their house looks amazing," Alecia informs us. "And there's way too much food for just the two of them."

"Will's probably already eaten most of it," Meg comments.

"I planned for him," Alecia replies. "I've been planning family events for five years. I've got this."

The guys have left the stage, and the crowd is chanting for an encore, which of course they'll get. Nash tickets might be out-of-this-world expensive, but the show is worth every dime.

"Thank you for bringing me to this," Wyatt murmurs in my ear. I grin up at him.

"Thanks for coming."

Will, Luke, and Dominic stayed at Sam's house for the concert. Will and Luke will draw attention away from the stage, and Dom volunteered to finish setting up so Alecia could come to the concert and enjoy the show.

Everyone else is here. I have no idea who got suckered into taking the dozen or so kids for the night, but I don't envy them.

That's a lot of kids. The Montgomerys reproduce like it's a job.

When the concert is officially over, and Nash has taken their bows, we make our way backstage.

"We can seriously just see them later," Jules says, but Sam shakes her head.

"He'll want to see us. Trust me."

We turn a corner as Leo does. He's clearly looking for someone, and the way his face lights up when he sees Sam says he's found her.

"Hey, sunshine," he says as he pulls her into his arms and kisses her soundly. "How were we?"

"So fucking good," she says before kissing him again. "I'm so proud of you."

He just hugs her close, then sets her down, and everyone else moves in for hugs and handshakes. When he gets to me, he surprises me by hugging me tightly.

"So glad you came, little one."

"Thanks for inviting me," I reply. "It was *so good*, Leo."

"I know," he says with a cocky wink, then turns his attention to Wyatt. "I'm Leo."

Wyatt just laughs. "Yes, I know. I'm Wyatt."

"*The* Wyatt?" he asks with a raised brow. "Well, we'll have to talk later, then."

Wyatt and I exchange surprised looks.

"Why do you all talk so much?" I ask the group at large.

"You're a Montgomery," my cousin, Caleb, reminds me. "This is not news."

"At least you'd never talk about me behind my back, Caleb."

"He doesn't talk to *anyone*," Jules reminds me.

"Exactly."

Caleb just winks at me, then gives Wyatt the stink eye again.

"Stop looking at him like that."

"I don't think we formally met earlier," Wyatt says and steps over to him. "I'm Wyatt Crawford."

"Are you just fucking her, or are you her boyfriend?" Caleb asks, making me gasp, Nat roll her eyes, and Brynna laugh.

This isn't funny.

Okay, it's kind of funny.

"We can't have this conversation now," Matt says. "The others aren't here to hear the answer."

"Save it then," Caleb says. "And think long and hard about that answer."

"MY COUSINS ARE stupid," I grumble in the car on the way to Sam and Leo's fortress on the cliff that overlooks the Pacific Ocean. "I mean, this is the twenty-first century, and they're acting like cavemen."

"They're acting like people who care about you. They don't know me," Wyatt reminds me and kisses my fingers. "We'll chat it out tonight."

"No fists," I warn him.

"I've never punched anyone," he says with a laugh.

"You were going to punch Archer the other day."

"Well, in my defense, he was touching you, and you were saying *no*. So, yeah, he might have seen the wrong side of my fist."

I study him as he turns off the freeway, following the directions on the GPS.

"You know what occurred to me yesterday?" I ask.

"What's that?"

"That you might have had a moment of déjà vu." I lick my lips. "From before."

"Like I said, it wasn't a good moment," he says, his jaw tense. I reach up and brush the backs of my fingers down his smooth cheek, wishing I could scoot into his lap and hold him close.

"I'm sorry. It didn't occur to me in the moment," I say quietly. "I just had my own déjà vu regarding my ex, and it irritated me."

He spares me a glance, his eyes warm in the darkness. "We're fine."

"I know." I shrug a shoulder. "But I'm still sorry."

"Don't worry about it," he says, turning right into the driveway and punching in the code at the gate that Sam texted me. He drives down and parks behind Luke's fancy Mercedes, kills the engine, and turns to me.

"Are we going in?"

"I want to say something first. We both need to make an effort to not jump to conclusions. To ask or talk before we assume the worst because of the shit we went through before."

"You're right." I nod and then decide, *fuck it*. I scoot across the center console and shimmy my way into his lap, making us both laugh. "This was much sexier in my head."

"It's not *not* sexy, but damn, you're going to make me hard, and I have to go behave around your family for a few hours before I can get you home."

"You'll be okay." My voice is confident as I wrap my arms around his neck and lean in, pressing my breasts against his chest. "We should shake on the whole talk before judging thing."

"This is shaking?" He cocks a brow, and his eyes are lit up with humor.

"This is sexy shaking," I confirm, wiggling on him. I can feel him begin to harden through his jeans and my panties.

"You know, all I have to do is unzip my pants and rip your underwear."

"See, there are those caveman tendencies again." I kiss him softly.

"You're *on* my cock, Amelia. I don't have any blood left in my brain."

I giggle and bury my face in the crook of his neck.

"I really just wanted to hold you for a minute."

"I'm holding *you*," he says, but his hands are rubbing up and down my back, not in a sexual kind of way, but as if to say, *"I've got you."*

"It's nice."

We're quiet for a moment until there's a knock on the window, making us both jump. Wyatt rolls down the window to find Jules standing there, laughing.

"No fucking in the car, guys. There's a party going on."

"We're not fucking," I inform her.

"Yet," Wyatt adds, making us laugh. "We'll be right behind you."

She nods and skips away, as Jules does. She's always seemed so light on her feet, so happy. She slips one arm through Nate's, and they make their way inside.

"We should go," I murmur. He frowns and looks as if he wants to say something else, but he just sighs.

"Let's do it."

He helps me off his lap and out of his door, then passes me my clutch and joins me. Sam and Leo's house is only a few years old. Leo had it built for her not long after they met. During the day, it has an impressive view of the ocean.

Once inside, we follow the noise to the back of the house where the party is set up. The kitchen and family rooms are open to each other. Huge doors open accordion-style out to the back terrace, making it one big indoor-outdoor space.

Alecia's crew has strung Edison lights everywhere, casting the space in a soft glow. She also added a few tables with chairs. The firepit is lit, music is piped through the space, and Maroon 5 is singing about sugar.

"This is stunning." Alecia is standing near the entrance to the terrace, smiling, holding her wine. Dominic is standing next to her, talking to Will.

"Thanks," she says, glancing around. "I think it's pretty. It's not necessary to go crazy when it's just the family, but this is a big deal. I don't know many people who wrap up a world tour every day."

"I'm kind of a big deal," Leo says as he joins us.

"I hear it was a great show," Will says, slapping Leo on the shoulder.

"It was fun. I'm exhausted," Leo says. "But I'm not the one we want to talk to."

All of their eyes shift to Wyatt, and I realize that all of the cousins have gathered around.

"Am I about to die?" Wyatt asks calmly.

"Depends on your answers," Will says with a shrug and shoves a chocolate cupcake into his mouth.

Whole.

Which just makes me laugh.

"This isn't funny," Caleb says.

"Yes, it is. Will is stuffing his face, and you guys are all acting like bullies."

"Bullies?" Matt asks, scowling. "We're not bullies. We're family."

"What would you like to know?" Wyatt asks, smiling at them. He doesn't look scared in the least.

He should be scared.

"Are you fucking her, or are you around for the long haul?" Caleb asks bluntly, crossing his arms over his chest. I look to Jules or Nat or Stacy for help, but they're just avidly watching.

"First of all," Wyatt begins, his voice calm with an edge to it. An edge I don't think I've heard before. "Her name is Amelia, and what I do with her when we're in private is consensual and none of your business. Secondly, I wouldn't be here if I was only interested in getting into her pants. And third, I'll be happy to be with her for as long as she wants me around.

"And one more thing, cousin or not, I'm not comfortable with you using such vulgar terms when referring to Amelia."

"What do you do for a living?" Dominic asks. Caleb's arms are at his sides again, and they've stopped glaring at him.

Progress.

"He's an architect," Matt says and then smiles. "I'm a cop. I checked you out."

"My brother's also a cop," Wyatt replies. "So, that doesn't surprise me."

"What's his name?"

"Levi."

Matt tilts his head to the side. "You're Crawford's brother?"

Wyatt nods.

"Well, shit. Why didn't you just say so? I've worked with Crawford for years."

I shake my head and look around the room. Am I in the *Twilight Zone*?

"How does this make sense to any of you?"

"It's a dude thing," Jules says with a shrug.

"I need wine." I turn to find Alecia already holding a glass out for me. "Thank God you guys own a vineyard. I'm going to need to drink it all."

She giggles and then looks at someone coming in behind me. "You guys made it!"

I turn to find Archer and Anastasia joining us, and I run to hug them.

"We both just finished up with work and didn't want to miss the party," Stasia says. "Did they already grill Wyatt?"

"Yes," I reply.

"Damn it, I missed it," Archer says.

"You grilled me the other day," Wyatt reminds him.

"I know, but they put on a hell of a show," Archer says with a laugh.

"Wait." I tug on Archer's sleeve. "You were alone with him for like one minute. How did you grill him?"

"Doesn't take long," my brother replies and goes off in search of beer.

"Men confuse me."

"Drink some more wine," Brynna suggests.

"SO, HE'S YOUR *neighbor*," Stacy says an hour later when she, Nic, and I are chatting by the firepit. We have wine and chips and queso.

It's perfect.

"Yep. He came over to introduce himself the day I moved in."

"He seems really nice," Stacy says with a smile.

"He is. Like, he's a *nice* guy, and those are hard to find."

"Tell me about it," Nic replies, shaking her head. "Until I met Matt, I thought nice guys were mythical creatures."

"And yet, here we are," Stacy says with a smile. "We found a whole pack of nice guys."

"How did you and Isaac meet, Stacy?" I ask.

"In school. I took one look into those Montgomery blue eyes, and I knew my life would never be the same."

"I do think you all can hypnotize people with your eyes," Nic agrees. "I've never seen eyes so blue. And for all of you to have them, it's crazy. Are you aliens?"

I laugh. "Yes, blue-eyed aliens. That's what we are. I guess the gene is just strong in the family."

"Well, it's hard to resist. And when you add in the kindness, the protectiveness, well . . ." Stacy shrugs. "I just knew I'd never be able to walk away from him."

I look over at Wyatt, who's currently talking with Will, Caleb, Archer, and Leo on the other side of the terrace. Will's making motions like he's throwing an imaginary football, so they're clearly talking about the sport.

Wyatt's laughing. He looks so at ease with them, as if he's known them all for years. Like they didn't just give him the third degree.

He fits here, with all of us. He fits in a way that no one else ever has. Vinnie certainly didn't, and that may be part of the reason that I didn't fight him on moving to L.A.

Archer slaps Wyatt on the shoulder, and they laugh again. Yes, he fits. With them, and with me.

"I'm glad you brought him," Nic says softly.

"Me, too."

"I missed all the good stuff the other night," Brynna says as she joins us. "I didn't get to chat with you guys, and I missed out on all of the makeup fun with Lia."

"I have so much more makeup to give you guys," I reply and make room for her next to me. "I'm telling you, it arrives *every day*. And there's no way that I'll ever be able to use all of it. You guys should put it to use.

Otherwise, it's just a waste."

"Well, we are not wasteful," Stacy says with a laugh.

"I need some book recommendations," I say to Stacy, who is a book reviewer. "I'm going to take advantage of sitting out by the pool with a book."

"I'll send you a list," she says with a nod.

"Lia!" Stasia comes running from inside. "Archer! We have to go. Something's wrong with Daddy."

"What?" I stand and rush to her. "What's wrong?"

"Mom just called and said they're on the way to the hospital in an ambulance. He collapsed and isn't waking up."

"Fuck," Archer mutters. "Let's go."

I glance around for Wyatt, but he's right next to me. "I have to go."

"We're going, baby."

"You'll drive?"

Why am I asking stupid questions? I feel like the floor just fell out from under me, and I can't get my bearings.

"Of course," he says and takes my hand. "Just text us with the address of where we're going."

Archer nods and glances around. "There's no need for you guys to wrap up the party. I'll call when we get there to let you know what's going on."

"We can be there in twenty minutes," Will reminds us. "Just call."

Anastasia is still on the phone with Mom, crying. She looks at me and shakes her head. "It's not good."

"Let's go," Wyatt says, leading me out to the car. "It's going to be okay."

I nod, feeling tears forming in my eyes.

It has to be okay.

eleven

Amelia

He had a heart attack.

That's really all we know right now. We're in the waiting room, outside of surgery while the surgeons are doing God knows what to my dad. Wyatt is sitting silently next to me, holding my hand. He's the only thing that's kept me from losing my shit. Archer is pacing the floor, talking to Matt on his phone, keeping them updated on the little we know.

Mom and Anastasia are sitting across from us, holding onto each other, looking as shell-shocked as I feel.

"Do you want some water?" Wyatt asks softly. I simply shake my head no and hold onto his hand tighter, leaning my head on his shoulder. Mom is watching us with sad eyes.

"I'll keep you posted." Archer hangs up the phone and drags his hand down his face. "How long is this going to take? They've been in there for two hours."

"They said it could take a while," Anastasia reminds him softly.

"I talked Steven and Gail out of coming down here until he's out of surgery. I'll call them when we know more."

"It's the not knowing that makes me crazy," I murmur. "Dad's healthy. I mean, sure, he likes his dessert, but he's always been fit. Now, suddenly, at sixty-five, he collapses of a heart attack?"

"His father died of a heart attack," Mom says and dabs a tear from the corner of her eye. I've never seen her look this deflated. This . . . *old.* "I assume it can be genetic."

We're quiet for a long moment. Wyatt shifts, wrapping his arm around my shoulders and kissing the top of my head.

He hasn't said much, but just having him next to me has been wonderful. Normally, I would tell him to go home so I could deal with this myself, but I haven't had that urge even once. I *need* him with me. A month ago, that would have sent me running in the other direction. I don't want to need anyone.

But it's different with him.

"I'm surprised Jace isn't the surgeon," I say to Wyatt.

"He's not on call tonight," he replies softly.

"I'm so glad you were in town," Anastasia says to me, and my eyes fill with tears. Oh my God, if I were still in L.A., I wouldn't have been here to be with my family. I wouldn't have been able to tell my dad that I love him and hug him, touch him.

I haven't even taken the time to see my dad since I've been here.

I *need* to move home.

"Me, too."

Before I can think about it further, the doctor walks into the room.

"Mrs. Montgomery?"

We all immediately stand, forming a circle around the doctor.

"He's stable. He had a massive heart attack, and had you not been there with him, he wouldn't have survived it."

Wyatt slips his hand into mine once again, holding on tightly.

"We placed two stents into arteries that were completely blocked. I'll show you those images in the morning when he's awake, and I can go through things more thoroughly."

"Where is he?" Mom asks.

"He's in recovery, and we'll have him in a room in ICU in about an hour. He will sleep through the night, so I suggest that all of you go home and get some rest."

"I'm not leaving," Mom insists. "So there better be a chair by his bed for me."

The doctor smiles kindly. "You can stay. The rest of you can see him in the morning."

"What time can we be here?" Wyatt asks, surprising me.

"Nine a.m. is when we open up for visitors," he replies and shakes our hands. "He's a lucky man."

With that, he walks away, and we all stand here for a moment, stunned, looking at each other.

"I'm staying with him," Mom says again.

"We'll come in the morning," Archer says. "We can take shifts with him if we can't all be in with him at once."

"He's going to be okay," I whisper and hang my head in my hands, hot tears running between my fingers. "Jesus, I was so scared."

"Hey, it's okay," Wyatt whispers, rubbing my back in circles. "Let's go home, sweetheart."

"All of you go home," Mom says. "You know I'll call if there are any changes."

I immediately cross to her and fold her into my arms. She feels smaller somehow, frailer, and I don't want to let go.

"I love you, Mama," I whisper.

"I love you, too, sweet girl," she replies softly. "Go rest up."

We say our goodbyes, and Archer insists on staying with Mom until she can join Dad. He looks tired. Worried.

"This is not how I thought we'd be ending the night," I say once we're in Wyatt's car and heading home.

"Me either," he says and sighs. "How are you?"

"Tired." I rest my elbow on the windowsill and lean my head on my hand as he rests his palm on my thigh. "Worried. A little sad."

"How can I help?"

I glance over at him and feel so fucking grateful. "You've done so much, Wyatt. Just having you with me is huge. You could have gone home at any time. Archer would have given me a ride home."

"No, I couldn't have left." His voice is harder now. "I'm not going to bail when it gets hard, Lia."

He rarely calls me Lia.

"That's not what I meant. I just would have understood, that's all. And I'm tired, so I'm saying the wrong things."

He pulls my hand up to kiss my knuckles. "Go to sleep for a bit."

But I don't sleep. I close my eyes and drift in and out, in that in-between place where you're still aware of what's happening around you, but you're a little dreamy, too. He's flipped on the radio, and Ed Sheeran is crooning softly to me.

The car comes to a stop, and I open my eyes, surprised to be in Wyatt's driveway instead of mine.

"You'll have to help me walk home. I might be stumbly."

"I want you in my bed tonight. I can take care of you here."

I frown. "You don't have to take care of me."

He rubs his forehead, right between his eyes. "Amelia, I understand that you're fierce and independent, but for God's sake, let me take care of you tonight."

I blink at him slowly and realize in this moment that I'm letting all of my walls fall with this man. It both terrifies me and fills me with hope.

"Okay." I nod and sit back, waiting for him to walk around and open my door. He helps me into the house and pauses at the stairs.

"Do you need anything?"

"Just you," I reply without thinking, and I'm suddenly swept up in his arms as he climbs the stairs. "You're really strong."

He smiles and kisses my forehead. "You're a little thing."

I just tuck my face into his neck as he carries me to the bedroom and sets me down carefully on the bed. He helps me slip my dress over my head, then surprises me by turning away for a moment and returning with one of his T-shirts.

Wordlessly, he tugs it over my head, pulls my hair through, and then literally tucks me into bed.

He wasn't lying when he said he wanted to take care of me.

"I'll be right back."

"I'm not broken. Dad's going to be okay."

He kisses my forehead and walks out of the room, then returns minutes later with two bottles of water, setting one on my nightstand

and the other on his.

The only light coming into the room is from the full moon through the balcony doors. Wyatt shucks his clothes, leaving his boxers on, and slides between the sheets, gathering me into his arms.

"This is really nice," I say softly.

"Just sleep, beautiful."

HE'S KISSING MY nipples.

My eyes open into slits, watching him nuzzle and kiss my breasts through his shirt. His hands are under it, sliding up my ribs, pushing the cotton out of the way to bare my skin, and my body is already heating up under his touch. I bury my fingers in his hair, and he smiles against me.

"I woke you up," he murmurs.

"In a spectacular fashion," I agree as he pushes the shirt up over my head and tosses it aside. His sheets are warm, but he's opened the balcony door, letting in the cool morning air, and it feels delicious.

The birds singing mixed with our heavy breathing are the only sounds as he nibbles his way across my torso. His fingers dip over my hip, just grazing my most sensitive center, making my hips buck, but then he's gone again, touching my legs and waist.

"Teasing me."

"Mm." He kisses my sternum, then up to my collarbone. "Savoring. Enjoying." He kisses my chin. "You're so beautiful, Amelia."

I cup his face in my hands as he presses the head of his cock against my core, pushing just slightly inside me.

"You completely undo me," he says as he slides home. "I don't remember what life was like before you, and I can't imagine going through a day without seeing you."

"Wyatt." I wrap my legs around his waist and hold on as he starts to move. He's kissing me now like his life depends on it, and in this moment, it just might.

He's moving in a slow, steady rhythm, cradling my head in his hands. I want to tell him that I love him, but the first time shouldn't be now when we're having crazy amazing sex. I don't want him to think that it's just in the heat of the moment.

It's too big for that.

His forehead is resting on mine as our hips move, the cool air swirling around us. His hazel eyes pin mine.

"I've never seen eyes so blue," he murmurs, rubbing his nose over mine. He takes my wrist and anchors it over my head, lifting my chest and giving him easier access to my nipple.

He wraps his lips around it, my hips arch, and that's it. I see stars, my world exploding spectacularly around us. Wyatt groans, falling over with me.

"Can't resist you," he murmurs, kissing my jawline, before rolling away. "Now, it's time to get up."

"You have a lot of energy this morning."

He grins. "It's going to be a busy day. Get up so we can get you dressed and to the hospital."

"Shit, my dad!" I sit up, frantically reaching for clothes. "I need to get to the hospital."

He rolls his eyes. "That's what I just said."

"You don't have to go with me. I know it's a workday."

"Let's not have this conversation again. I'll go with you, and if things are good, I don't have to go again, but I *want* to be there for you, Amelia."

"Thank you." I check my phone. "No news is good news, right?"

He nods, watching me, and I can't help but reach out and brush his hair off of his forehead. "Thank you. For everything."

He plants his hand on my ass, giving it a little squeeze. "You're welcome."

"HOW'S YOUR DAD?" Jules asks the next day. We're at lunch on the waterfront, enjoying a Friday afternoon in the sunshine.

"He's doing much better. He should be able to go home tomorrow. I was at the hospital this morning, and he was *grouchy*. I apologized to the nurses for his behavior."

"I'm sure he's ready to go home," she says with a laugh. "Men aren't good patients."

"To be fair, I'm not either. I had my appendix out about five years ago, and I wasn't a delight. I must get it from my dad." I shrug and take a bite of my chicken and avocado sandwich.

"Do they know what caused it?"

"Well, yeah. He doesn't eat as well as he should, but they think it mostly stems from genetics. Mom will be on him to eat better, and he'll be on medication for the rest of his life."

"And how are *you*?" she asks. "Any news from L.A?"

"Not in about a week," I reply, wiping my mouth. "We're still waiting. I'm so over this, Jules. It's frustrating."

"I know. How are the makeup people taking it?"

"It cost them some money to put the launch on hold, but so far, they've been understanding. They moved the release date to late fall, so it should be in stores by Christmas."

"That's still good," Jules assures me.

"I know, I'm just impatient."

"I'm sure you're ready to go home and get back to your life."

I stare at the French fry in my hand for a long minute. "Actually, I've been thinking. I don't miss L.A. like I thought I would. I have some friends that I miss, but honestly, I just don't think I fit down there anymore."

"What are you saying?" She's staring at me with so much hope, it gives me excited butterflies.

"I think I want to move home. The other night when we were at the hospital, I just kept thinking that if this had happened when I was in California, I could have lost my dad without being able to be here with him. I miss my family, all of my family. Even though your brothers are overprotective and drive me mad, I love them. I love all of you."

"We love you, too," Jules says. "And trust me, I get it. I thought Caleb was going to kill Nate the first time they met."

"I only have one protective brother. I don't know how you do it with five of them."

"I don't either," she says with a laugh. "But they mean well. And we all just want what's best for you. Have you talked to your family about it?"

"No, I don't want to get their hopes up in case it doesn't happen. But I'm ninety-nine percent sure it's going to happen."

"This is so exciting!" She dances in her seat. "What does Wyatt think? He must be excited, too."

"I haven't talked to him yet, either." I shift in my seat. "That's a whole different conversation."

"Oh, are you ready to break it off? I thought you guys looked so happy the other night."

"No." The thought of breaking it off makes me sick to my stomach. "It's not that. Jules, I think I'm in love with him."

"Okay."

She's watching me as if I'm about to drop some bombshell. "That's it. I'm in love with him."

"That's awesome."

"Is it?"

"Okay, you're confusing me." She sets her empty plate aside and sips her iced tea. "You're in love, with the opportunity to move home. Why is this bad again?"

"I'm so confused." I hang my head and rub my hands over my thighs in agitation. "It's not that it's bad. But it's scary. I did the love thing once, and it turned out horribly. I trusted him, I loved him, the sex was great. And then it went to hell in a handbasket."

"So you think it'll happen again." She nods, thinking it over. "I mean, there's no guarantee that it won't, Lia."

"That is not encouraging."

"But you've been through the bad, and you know what signs to look for. Is Wyatt like Vinnie?"

"Not even in the same wheelhouse."

"Well, there you go. You can't judge Wyatt based on what you've been through before him. Have you said it yet?"

"No. That's the other thing. It doesn't seem fair to tell him I love him when I could turn around and move away."

"But you're ninety-nine percent sure you're moving to Seattle."

"There's still that one percent. And I don't want him to think that I'm moving here just for him. That's a lot of pressure, and it's not true."

She narrows her eyes at me. "What are you afraid of?"

"Getting my heart broken," I admit right away. "Wyatt is, well, he's everything I thought I'd never find. He's amazing. And what if he decides that I'm not amazing and he bails?"

"Not gonna happen. Sweetie, you didn't see the way he was looking at you the other night. He couldn't take his eyes off of you. And when my brothers grilled him, and he replied with *it's none of your business*? Yeah, that was hot."

"Totally hot," I agree.

"He loves you, too, even if he hasn't been able to say it either. You're on the same page."

"I wish I was as sure as you are."

"It's early days yet," she assures me. "You can give it more time. Relationships aren't a race."

"You don't have my mother hassling you for grandkids."

Jules tips her head back and laughs. "True. But still, it's really none of her business either. Give it time, say it when it's right. You'll know."

"You always were really smart."

"I know." She winks at me and picks up the dessert menu. "I really want something lemony. Will you share with me?"

"Of course. Also, back to moving here, do you think Nat and Luke would let me stay in the house until I find my own place? It shouldn't take long, and I'd be happy to pay rent."

"Oh, I can't see why not. You should just go over and talk to them. They're awesome."

"Luke intimidates me. Even more than Nate."

She cocks a brow. "Really? That's awesome. I can't wait to tell Nate."

"Don't tell him!"

"Why not? He thinks he's so intimidating."

"Well, he is. But there's just something about Luke that makes me nervous."

"He's a really nice guy." She tips her head and frowns. "I don't think he has a mean bone in his body."

"It's not that." I shake my head, trying to put my finger on it. "It could be because he's so fucking hot, he could set the sun on fire."

"There's that," Jules says. "And maybe because he's a movie star?"

"Maybe. I don't know. But you're right, I'm silly. He's great, and I'll go talk to them about it this week."

"Lia! I'm so excited! You're going to live here. We need to celebrate right now with some shopping."

"Well, I'll never turn that down."

SHOPPING IS MY happy place. Rachel, our sales associate at the Chanel boutique in Neiman Marcus, is an enabler, God bless her.

Both my and Jules' cars are full of happy purchases.

I should head home right away. Wyatt and I have plans for dinner, and I still need to get ready, but something tells me to swing back by the hospital to see Dad one more time today.

The fact that he's going to make a full recovery is a blessing, and I want to say goodnight. It shouldn't take long.

"Hey there, poodle," he says when he sees me in the doorway. He's in the hospital gown and his own sweatpants from home, with his slippers.

"I always hated that nickname," I reply and cross to him, sitting in the chair my mom's been in for three days.

"Why do you think I always kept using it?" He winks at me and reaches out for my hand. "I'm happy you're here."

"Where's Mom?"

"I talked her into going home for a shower and a change of clothes. I lied and told her she smelled bad."

"She loves you, Dad."

He smiles, the way he always has when he speaks of my mom. "And I love her, but the woman hovers, Amelia."

I laugh and kiss his rough hand. "That she does. Are you being nicer to the nurses?"

"Speaking of hovering," he mutters.

"You had a heart attack, Dad."

"I was there," he reminds me. "But, yes. That nice little brunette took me out for some fresh air, and that helped me feel better."

"That was nice of her," I reply. "Looks like they'll be springing you free in the morning."

"Thank God," he says. "This bed is hard as a rock, and they have me eating cardboard."

"It's a heart-healthy menu."

He scowls. "A salt shaker wouldn't kill them."

I sigh and roll my eyes. "I just wanted to stop by to say goodnight before I head home. Do you want me to come up tomorrow morning when they discharge you?"

"No, your mom will be here. I'll text you when I'm home."

"Well, hello there."

I turn at what sounds like Wyatt's voice, but it's Jace, in a white coat with a stethoscope around his neck.

"Hi, Dr. Crawford," I reply, making him grin.

"You can call me Jace just about everywhere," he says with a smile. "Your dad's doing great."

He spends the next ten minutes filling us in on his most recent blood work and EKG, and when he's done, I'm surprised when he says, "Want to grab a quick bite in the cafeteria?"

"Do you know each other?" Dad asks, hope in his blue eyes, and I can't help but laugh.

"I'm actually dating Jace's brother," I reply, catching the grin on Dad's face. "Sure, that would be great, Jace. Just give me a minute."

I say goodbye to Dad, and Jace is waiting for me at the nurse's station when I walk out.

"I have a break," he says. "And, honestly, I'd like to get to know you a little better."

"Likewise. Let me just text Wyatt."

Hey! Sorry, I got hung up at the hospital. Everything is okay, but I think I'm going to miss dinner.

When we're in the elevator, Wyatt replies.

No worries, I'm swamped with work. See you tomorrow?

I grin. *Yes. I'll be around all day!*

"Is he mad?" Jace asks.

Sleep well, sweetheart.

"No, he's busy tonight anyway." I tuck my phone into my handbag and follow Jace through the cafeteria, choosing a salad and a bottle of water. We find a seat by a wall of windows that looks out across the city. "This is actually pretty nice."

"And the food isn't bad," he agrees, shaking his bottle of chocolate milk. "Protein."

"So, how is Dad, really?"

He frowns. "He's going to be fine."

"But you're not going to tell me the nitty-gritty."

He shakes his head. "There are laws, Amelia."

"I'm his daughter."

"Not his wife," he reminds me. "But I'm not lying when I say that he's going to be fine."

"It was scary."

"I know." He takes a bite of his burger.

"How do you eat like that and still look the way you do?"

"And how do I look?" he asks with a grin.

"All three of you look like you walked out of an action movie."

He laughs. "I've never heard that one before. I'm claiming Thor."

"That's what *she* said."

He laughs again. "I burn a lot of calories every day. We are blessed with fast metabolisms."

"No kidding."

"So, I'm going to get to the nitty-gritty of why I asked you here," he says, using the words I did a moment ago.

"Okay."

"My brother is invested. I can see it in the way he looks at you, and you're spending a lot of time together."

"Is this where you threaten me about breaking his heart?"

His eyes narrow. "No. He's an adult, and he's no fool. Despite what

Cruella pulled. I guess I'm curious if it's reciprocated."

"The investment?"

He nods.

"It is." I sigh and set my fork down. "We're both spending a lot of time together. I think we're bad for each other's productivity. At least, he has been for mine. It's a good thing I'm self-employed."

I prop my chin in my hand.

"Yeah, the investment is mutual."

A slow smile spreads over Jace's face. The Crawford men are sexy, I'll give them that.

"Good."

"Are you going to eat all of your fries?" I ask.

"Help yourself."

twelve

Wyatt

It's early Saturday morning, and I've already been in my office for an hour. Since I've been seeing Amelia, my work has slipped back a peg on my priority list, and I have a massive amount to catch up on. My partners aren't pleased.

They aren't pissed. No one has had to pick up my slack, and they won't have to. But I'm not as available as I usually am, and rather than being way ahead of deadline, I'm rushing to meet them.

That's not how I work.

Amelia is the priority right now, and that's not going to change, but I need to find the balance between work and my love life.

I never expected to have this problem. It's not a bad one in the least.

I'm finishing some changes to the outdoor space on a project when my phone rings.

"Hey," I say to my brother.

"What's up?" Jace asks.

"I'm working. Isn't it early for you? You're not a morning person."

"I haven't been home yet. I was on last night and ended up working on an emergency quadruple bypass."

"Jesus," I mutter and push my fingers into my eyes. "Just the words are exhausting."

"Tell me about it." He yawns. "I'm driving home now and wanted to give you a quick call. I spent some time with Amelia last night."

I frown, looking up from my computer.

"You what?"

"She was at the hospital, and I spent some time with her. I really like her, Wyatt. I had a good feeling about her after we had dinner together, but after spending some one-on-one time with her, I think she's really great."

I'm still scowling at *one-on-one time*.

"How much time did you spend?"

"Why do you sound like that? She texted and told you she was hung up at the hospital."

"Yeah, she did." I clear my throat and stand to pace my office. "I'm glad you like her. I like her, too."

"Anyway, that's all I was calling about, not that it matters."

"It matters," I reply. "Go get some sleep."

I hang up, toss my phone on the desk, and shove my hands into my pockets, turning to stare at Amelia's house across the street.

So, she wasn't just spending time with her dad last night. She missed dinner because she was with Jace.

I trust them both. I *know* this is not Claudia, and that she wasn't boning a friend of mine. Or a stranger, for that matter.

She was just hanging out with my brother.

I trust them.

But I'm completely irritated at the situation.

It's still early enough in the day that there's no one out and about. The sun has just come up. So, I put Amelia, my brother, and all of my feelings into a box so I can sit down and get some damn work done.

I'll see her later and calmly talk to her about last night.

Rationally.

I'M NOT FEELING rational yet. I was able to get most of the work done that I wasn't able to get to during the week. Amelia texted when she woke up to say hi, and then again about thirty minutes ago to tell me she's free for a while.

So, I'm walking across the street, slower than I normally would, my hands in my shorts' pockets.

I'm not sure what to say or how to bring it up.

Because any way that I run through it in my head, I sound like a jerk.

"Hey," she says with a bright smile when she opens the door. She grabs my hand, pulls me inside, and reaches up on her tiptoes to kiss me. "How are you?"

"I'm good," I reply, some of my irritation evaporating. "You look fantastic."

"I just filmed a video," she says with a grin. "This is my everyday look."

"I like it." She kisses me again, then leads me through the kitchen. "I can't get enough of the pool. I hope you don't mind sitting out there for a while."

"Not at all."

She happily leads me to a chaise lounge big enough for two. I sit, and she joins me, snuggling close.

"My dad went home this morning," she says. "He was better last night when I saw him. Not nearly as grouchy."

"That's good. How does he feel?"

"Pretty good, from what he says. Mom will take care of him. I went shopping with Jules yesterday."

She tells me all about her shopping trip, what she bought, and I try to follow along, but she's talking quickly. She's happy today.

"Oh, I saw Jace."

"I heard."

She glances up at me and frowns. "Why do you say it like that?"

I sigh, drag my hand down my face and shake my head. "No reason."

"Oh, no. There's a reason." She shifts, sitting next to me cross-legged. "It's written all over your ridiculously handsome face. What's up? We just had dinner."

I lick my lips, trying to figure out how to say what I have to say without sounding like a dick or a petulant child. "You were supposed to have dinner with me."

"But I didn't stand you up. I texted to let you know that I wasn't going to make it."

"So you could have dinner with my brother instead."

She tilts her head to the side and narrows her eyes. "Seriously? You're jealous of your brother?"

"I'm not jealous," I reply and stand to pace. "And this might be a good time to remind you that you were jealous of your sister the first time I met her."

"*Nothing* happened," she says.

"I know that," I immediately reply. "I trust you. Both of you."

"Then what is this about?" She looks as confused as I feel.

I shake my head and hold my hands out at my side. "It's clearly nothing."

"No." She stands now and marches to me. "You're the one who said we need to talk to each other so we don't let our baggage fuck this up. It works both ways, Wyatt. If I've pissed you off, I need to know *why.*"

"That's just it, it's *baggage.* You shouldn't have to deal with it."

"But you don't like that I had dinner with your brother."

"No. I don't like it."

"So, let me be real with you right now. The fact that you don't like it triggers my own damn baggage. So your baggage is going to keep triggering my baggage, and we'll stay in this circle of frustration forever. And I can't do that, Wyatt. So what do you propose we do?"

"I don't know how long I have with you," I blurt out and shove my hands into my pockets again. I want to reach for her, but not yet. I need to say this. "And the not knowing sucks, Amelia. We were supposed to have dinner last night, and you canceled so you could spend the evening with my brother instead."

"So, you don't think we did anything inappropriate, you just don't like that I used my time that way."

"Correct."

"And that pisses me off because my ex liked to dictate who I could and couldn't spend my time with."

"That's not what this is." I pace away in frustration and push my hands through my hair. "I don't care if you have dinner with the whole cast of *Friends* and *Oprah*, Lia."

"I would enjoy that, actually."

"Spend all day with my whole family if you want, but damn it, I want to be included in that."

"Your feelings are hurt," she says and covers her mouth with her hand, her blue eyes wide.

I sigh again and hang my head. "I hadn't thought of it that way, but that could be what this is. I don't know."

"Wyatt, I don't ever want to hurt your feelings."

"Hey, guys!" Natalie walks into the pool area, carrying her camera, followed by two guys. They're holding hands, grinning.

Clearly about to have sexy photos taken.

"Sorry to interrupt," Nat continues. "I'll be working in the studio for a few hours."

"It's fine," I reply and walk toward the doors. "I honestly have to get back to work."

"Wyatt, I'll come with you and we—"

"No." I shake my head. "It's okay. I'm behind on work and just took a break to come see you for a few minutes."

"I don't want to leave it like this," Amelia says softly after Nat and the men disappear into the studio. "I'll come with you, and we can talk."

"I think I need a breather," I reply, and her eyes widen again.

"Like, a forever breather?"

"No." I pull her to me and hug her close. "A for today breather. I have work, Amelia. I promise I'm not lying about that. I have a Monday deadline that I'm behind on. And I know that I've been keeping you away from work, too."

"I have some work to do," she confirms. "But I hate letting you leave like this. I didn't mean to hurt your feelings."

"I know." I kiss her forehead and then her lips. "I'll see you tomorrow."

She nods and lets me go.

JESUS, IT'S BEEN a long fucking day.

Productive, but long.

My back aches from sitting for too many hours in this godforsaken chair, and my head hurts from staring at the computer. I've been on the phone more than I like today, and didn't eat anything to speak of. Unless coffee is considered a meal, in which case, I had about six of them.

But, I'm fully caught up, and even ahead for the week to come. It feels good. I turn the computer off and rub my eyes. I'm exhausted. Sleeping for a week sounds like a great idea.

But first, a shower.

I grab my phone and notice that I've missed a text from Amelia. I've been so engrossed in work, I didn't even hear it.

Hey. I've been thinking about you a lot today. I feel bad about the way we left things. Please tell me that you know that I didn't mean to hurt your feelings.

I smile and type out a reply. *I know you didn't mean to. We'll talk about it tomorrow. I promise.*

I leave the office and head upstairs to my bedroom. My feet feel heavy. My phone pings with an immediate response from Amelia.

I was hoping we could discuss it tonight, but it's late, and I'm already in bed.

I quickly peel off my clothes, start the water, and reply to her.

I'm exhausted, sweetheart. We should both get some rest and talk tomorrow when our heads are clear.

I reach for a clean towel, hang it on the rack, and just as I'm about to step under the water, she replies.

Goodnight. She follows it up with a sleepy emoji, and my heart swells. Part of me wants to say screw it and run over to hold her and talk everything out with her tonight. But I'm so fucking tired, I can barely keep my eyes open, and exhaustion wins.

The shower is a balm to my sore body. I'm not this tight and sore after working out with Jace for an hour, and that man is an animal. No more getting so behind on work that I have to do this again.

After I shut off the taps and dry myself, I pull on a T-shirt and pair of gym shorts, then head downstairs for a bottle of water. I notice my office light is still on, so I swing through to shut it off.

Before I turn to leave, I notice a flash above Amelia's house. Expecting it to be lightning, I walk to the windows, looking closer. There's nothing for a long moment, and I begin to think that it was just a figment of my tired brain, but then it happens again.

Except, that's not lightning.

It's fire.

Amelia's house is on fucking fire.

My heart slams into my throat as I run out of the house, desperate to get to her. I pound on the door, but she doesn't open it. She's not outside. The smell of fire and falling ash hangs around me.

She must be asleep.

"Wake up, baby." I bang on the door again, pounding with the flat of my fist, but she still doesn't come outside. I look in the front windows, but the house is dark.

I have to get in there. I told her we would talk tomorrow, and what if tomorrow is too late? What if I don't get the chance to tell her that I love her?

What in the hell have I done?

I race back to my own garage, calling 911 on my way. I need shoes.

"911, what's your emergency?"

"A house fire," I reply, panting heavily. I rattle off the address. "I can't see where it's coming from, but the flames are coming over the house. And my girlfriend is still inside."

"She's in the house, sir?"

"Yes." My heart is in my throat as I reach for a sledgehammer and shove my feet into my yard-working shoes. "She's not opening the door. I'm going to bust the window in to get to her."

"Sir, do not enter the house. Help is on the way. I need you to stay away from the building."

I hang up on her. Fuck that. I won't stay away from the house. The woman I love more than anything is in there, and it's on fucking fire.

I run back over and bust the front window open easily. I can hear sirens in the distance as I climb over the glass.

"Amelia!"

There's no smoke inside the house, which fills me with relief. Now, where the hell is she?

thirteen

Amelia

I sit up in bed with a start. I swear someone just broke a window.

Someone is breaking into this house!

"Amelia!"

It's Wyatt. I throw on a T-shirt and shorts and meet him at the top of the dark stairs.

"Wyatt? What's wrong? Did you break the window?"

"Are you okay?" He cups my face. His eyes are wild in the moonlight, and suddenly, I realize there's light dancing on the walls.

"Of course. What's going on?"

"The house is on fire. Come on, we need to go."

"I need to grab my purse."

"Lia." He stares at me like *really?* but I just run back to the bedroom, grab my purse, and before I can slide my feet into flip-flops, he slings me over his shoulder and carries me down the stairs and out the front door.

He sets me down, and I immediately run around the house, Wyatt on my heels.

"Stop, Amelia. I called 911."

"I hear them." And I can smell the fire. I need to know where it is. Have I just burned Natalie's house down? I round the corner of the house to find Natalie's studio ablaze and reach out blindly for Wyatt. "Holy fuck."

"I don't want you back here," he says, pulling me toward the street. "It's dangerous. Come on, baby."

"The studio is on fire." I'm not moving, and Wyatt takes my face in his hands again, making me face him.

"Look at me, goddamn it! You're not safe here. Let's go."

I blindly follow him back to the street where fire trucks and an ambulance have pulled up, and the next three minutes are a blur of men running with hoses to the back of the house, and Wyatt and me watching from the safety of his driveway.

"Let's go inside."

"No," I reply, shaking my head, my feet hurting a bit from the rocks on the driveway. "I need to call Nat. And I need to make sure that I haven't burned her house down."

"You didn't do anything," he murmurs. His hands are rubbing up and down my arms soothingly. His voice is strong and reassuring.

God, I love this man. It's torn me apart all day that I could have hurt his feelings last night.

But I have to table that for later.

The guy who seems to be in charge jogs over to us.

"Do you live here?" he asks.

"I do, but I'm not the homeowner. I'm about to call her. What's happened?"

He scratches his cheek and props his hands on his hips. "It started in the guest house out back. We have it out now, but we're going to keep working on it in case it's burning below ground."

"Do you know how it started?" Wyatt asks.

"Not yet," he replies. "We'll be here for a while."

"I'll call Natalie," I say as the fireman walks away. I dial her number and squeeze my eyes shut. She might not be awake.

"Hello," she says on the second ring. She sounds wide-awake.

"Hey, Nat, it's Lia. I don't want to freak you out, but there's been a fire here at the house."

"Oh my God, Lia, are you okay?" There's rustling around, and I hear Luke talking in the background. "There's been a fire," she says to him.

"I'm fine. It wasn't in the house, it was out back in the studio."

"Well, thank God for that," she says. "Luke's calling his mom to come be with the kids, and I'm getting dressed. We'll be there soon."

"I'm so sorry, Nat."

"For what? You're not an arsonist. Accidents happen, I'm just so relieved that you're okay."

"I'm fine. I'll see you soon."

She ends the call, and I spin to wrap my arms around Wyatt, suddenly exhausted and relieved at once.

"Hey, you're okay, sweetheart."

"I know, I just feel so bad that it happened when I was here. They're on their way."

"Good. Now, look at me."

I do as he asks, and there's so much intensity looking down at me, I don't know what to say.

"That scared the life out of me." His voice is gruff. "Amelia, I'm so in love with you, I can't see straight. If I'd lost you tonight, I don't know what I would have done. The thought of it is a punch in the gut."

"I'm okay," I assure him and cup his face in my hands. "I'm right here, and I'm safe."

"I saw those flames over the house, and I swear, I've never been so terrified. I couldn't get to you fast enough, and then you weren't answering the door."

"I took a sleeping pill," I admit and bite my lip. "I knew I wouldn't sleep well because I was upset about our argument, so I took something. I didn't hear anything until you broke the window."

"If I hadn't seen it, it could have spread to the house," he says, his eyes closing in anguish. "I almost didn't come downstairs, Amelia. Jesus."

"But you did, and I'm fine, and the fire is out. It's out, Wyatt." I rub my thumbs over his cheeks. "Thank you for coming after me."

He jerks me against him, holding me closely and rocking us back and forth as organized chaos continues across the street. They're yelling orders, running about. But all I can concentrate on is this amazing man who's holding me as if I'm the most precious thing in his life.

He loves me.

I'm about to start talking about today and tell him that I love him, too, when Nat and Luke pull into Wyatt's driveway.

"Hey, guys," I say and suddenly find myself engulfed in a massive Nat hug.

"Are you sure you're okay?" she asks.

"Mmph fnnn."

She pulls back. "What?"

"I'm fine. But your studio isn't." I look around for the fireman who spoke with us earlier and point at him. "That's the guy in charge."

"I'm going to go have a talk with him," Luke says. His hair is standing on end, and he looks tired.

And hot. Luke always looks hot.

Because he's Luke Williams.

"I'll come with you." Nat squeezes my hand and then follows Luke to speak with the fireman. A few minutes later, they return. "He says that the main house is safe, but he'd like for us to stay out of it for tonight. But the studio is a loss."

"Oh, Nat, that sucks. I'm sorry."

She shrugs. "I can replace it all, Lia. But we can't replace you, so I'm relieved that you're okay."

"Wyatt saw the flames," I inform them and fill them in on how he broke the window to get to me.

Speaking of hot.

"I'll replace the window," Wyatt says, but Luke shakes his head.

"No, you won't. I would have done the same. Your leg is bleeding."

We all look down, and sure enough, he's cut and bleeding down into his shoe.

"I hadn't noticed," Wyatt says with a shrug. "Adrenaline."

"We have to get you stitched up," I reply, only to have him chuckle.

"I don't need stitches."

"Well, now that we know what's going on, we're going to head home and come back in the morning," Natalie says and hugs me again. Luke does the same, and I pat his back awkwardly, the way I always do when Luke hugs me.

Because he intimidates the hell out of me.

He gives me a smile, shakes Wyatt's hand, and they're off.

"Let's go in now," Wyatt says, taking my hand in his and pressing his lips to my knuckles. His eyes have calmed down, and he's gazing at me with love-filled hazel orbs.

The man might have hung the moon as far as I'm concerned.

"First stop is wherever you keep your first-aid kit, Captain America," I say as we walk inside.

"Captain America?"

"You're clearly an action movie star," I reply and smile when he smirks. "You legit broke a huge window and jumped through it, with your big muscles."

"It was pure adrenaline and needing to get to you," he says.

"Action movie star," I repeat with a nod. "Now, let this damsel in distress clean you up."

"You're not a damsel, but I'll let you clean me up." He leads me into the guest bedroom on the first floor, pulls a little box out of the lower cabinet, and passes it to me. "Here you go."

"This is all you have?" I stare at the little box in disbelief. "I'll be lucky to get a Band-Aid out of this."

"We're not doing major surgery here," he reminds me. "It's already done bleeding; we just have to clean it up."

"Okay." I start the water to heat it up, then rummage around for a washcloth. "Sit on the tub."

"Yes, ma'am." He does as I ask, and pulls his shoes off, then props his foot on the vanity and watches as I get my tools lined up. "Jace would be proud of your professionalism."

I swallow and wet the washcloth, then start at his ankle, cleaning the blood off. "Speaking of Jace," I murmur, not looking him in the eyes. Not yet. "Let's multi-task, shall we?"

"If you like."

"So, now that we've both had time to take a step back and let the frustration cool off, I have a couple of things to say."

"Shoot," he says, then hisses through his teeth when I wipe off the cut on his calf.

"Sorry." I wrinkle my nose. "Are you sure you don't want to go to the ER?"

"I'm not going to the ER for a cut on my leg," he replies, his voice as dry as sand. "You're doing great."

"Okay. Anyway. I want to apologize again because the thought of hurting your feelings, ever, makes my stomach sick. I would never do that on purpose."

He takes my hand in his, and I look into his eyes.

"I know, Amelia. You don't need to apologize, because you didn't do it on purpose."

"I still feel bad," I reply, blinking away tears. "But, you need to know that we didn't do anything wrong. I'm not attracted to Jace romantically. He's your brother, and I think he's a nice guy, and maybe we'll be friends. That's it."

"I know," he says softly as I gently rub some ointment on the cut, then reach for a bandage. "I realize that I overreacted. Like I said earlier, I trust you both. I would just rather you spent time with me rather than an ugly dude who doesn't deserve your company."

I laugh and put the first-aid kit away, then wash my hands and look up in the mirror to find Wyatt standing behind me and looking at me.

He's so fucking handsome. His hair is also wild, a little longer and darker than Luke's. His eyes are always so intense when he looks at me.

And that tattoo . . . well, it does things to me.

He wraps his arms around me from behind and holds my gaze in his. "Are we okay?" he asks.

"We're okay," I confirm, but then frown. "But, Wyatt, you were right before. We *have* to learn to talk to each other because, otherwise, our ghosts will ruin us, and I don't want that."

I turn in his arms and smile when his hands roam from my back to my ass.

"I'm being serious."

"I can be serious and still grab your ass," he replies, then tips his forehead against mine in that sweet way he does.

"I love you," I say, just blurting it out before I lose my nerve, and he pulls his head back, his eyes pinned to mine again. "I love you, Wyatt. I've wanted to say it for a while, but the timing was wrong."

"If I've learned anything tonight, it's that life is too precious to wait," he says, his lips just inches away from mine. "And I love you, too. Fuck the timing."

"THIS IS MY owl," Olivia, Nat's daughter says to me the next day. I've come to their house to talk to them about the possibility of staying at the house longer.

"It's a beautiful owl," I say to the adorable five-year-old. She has dark hair and green eyes, just like her mama. I mean, Luke and Natalie are two of the most beautiful people on the planet, so of course, their children are gorgeous. "What's her name?"

"Owlivia," she says with a giggle. "Do you see what I did there?"

I laugh as the girl sits next to me, as if she's at home here. "I do see what you did. Well, I think it's awesome."

"She doesn't have any babies," she informs me, her face suddenly serious. "But I have three babies."

"She's big into siblings these days," Luke says as he walks into the kitchen and makes a cup of coffee. "Would you like some?"

"No, thanks, I've had mine already."

"I'll take some, though," Nat says as she breezes in, looking fantastic as if she hadn't spent half of the night worried about a house fire.

"You need to eat, too," he reminds her before kissing her square on the mouth.

"Daddy kisses Mommy all the time," Olivia informs me. "Auntie Jules says it's gross."

"Do you think it's gross?"

She just giggles and shakes her head no. "It's because Daddy loves Mommy."

"That's right." I kiss her smooth cheek. "So, first of all, the clean-up crew was already in the backyard this morning. You move fast."

"I have work to do," Nat says with a shrug. "Were they there too early bugging you?"

"No, I was already up," I reply. "And I was at Wyatt's anyway. I just stopped over there to get fresh clothes and stuff. And, I have a favor to ask."

Luke passes Natalie a plate of fresh fruit, and they both turn their attention to me.

"What's up?" Luke asks, and I'm suddenly tongue-tied. Why can't I just talk to Natalie? It would be so much easier. "Actually, let me ask you this first. Have I offended you somehow?"

My head whips up, and I frown. "No, of course not. Why?"

"You seem uncomfortable around me, and I want to make sure that I didn't do something wrong."

"No." I shake my head and then laugh. "Honestly, you make me insanely nervous."

Natalie grins at him and chews on a strawberry. "Told you."

"I don't know why, because you've always been nice to me, Luke. But you might be one of the only people I've ever met who makes my palms sweat."

A slow smile spreads over his ridiculously handsome face. "Is it the movies?"

"Maybe? Mostly, I think it's just that you're hot. And I mean that in the most respectful way possible."

"No, I get it," Natalie says with a helpful nod. "He's totally hot."

"Does Daddy have a fever?" Olivia asks in my lap, making us all laugh.

"No, sweetie," I reply. "He's fine."

"Can we move past this nervousness?" Luke asks me. "Maybe you just haven't been around me enough to realize that despite the debonair good looks, charming smile, and classy ways, I'm just a normal man."

"And, here we go," Nat says, rolling her eyes. "You've given him a big head."

I laugh and shrug a shoulder. "Yes, we'll get past it. I'll wear gloves when I'm near you."

"What's the favor?" Natalie asks.

"Well, if I were to decide to move home permanently, would it be possible to rent the house from you until I find a place of my own?"

Natalie sets her plate down and claps her hands excitedly. "Of course! And you don't need to pay us, silly. You can stay as long as you want."

"Absolutely," Luke replies, nodding and smiling.

"I really don't mind paying rent. This house is in a prime location and could be bringing in a lot of income for you."

"It's convenient for the family," Nat says, waving me off. "Are you really going to move home?"

"I think so, yes. I have some things to tie up in L.A., and my new business venture will be out of there, so I'll have to commute a bit—"

"I do the same," Luke says with a nod. "It can be a pain, I'm not going to lie, but it's doable, and being near family makes the hassle worth it."

"That's what I'm thinking," I agree. "I've missed everyone, and with Dad's scare last week, I just think that it's time to be home."

"Well, you won't get an argument from me," Nat says. "I suspect a certain handsome architect had a hand in this decision?"

"No." I shake my head, but Nat just cocks a brow. "Well, partly. I haven't told him yet."

"Might want to," Luke suggests. "The man's a goner over you."

"We said the L word last night," I confess and then shake my head in bewilderment. "I definitely didn't expect to find him when I came here last month. I just wanted to work and be with the family. But here he is, and this may sound so incredibly cheesy, but he's totally changed my life. Turned it upside down, that's for sure."

"Love does that," Natalie says, looking at Luke. "He came out of nowhere on the beach and accosted me."

"I didn't *accost* you," he says with a laugh.

"You were ready to smash the hell out of my camera," she reminds him.

"I thought she was the press," he says to me.

"But I was just taking pictures of the sunrise," she adds. "And once he believed that I wasn't trying to get rich off of photos of him, he didn't let me out of his sight."

"I mean, look at her," he says with a smile, his arms crossed over his chest, and hip leaning against the countertop.

"Jules is right. Y'all are a little disgusting."

fourteen

Amelia

"D o you need all of that?" Wyatt asks a week later as I gather my things to go out of town with him for a few days. Jules and Nate invited us to go to their beach house on the coast, and I couldn't be more excited. Our trip to Orcas Island was fun and new, but the Washington coast is my home away from home, and I haven't been out there for a few years.

I'm practically giddy.

"I don't understand the words coming out of your mouth," I reply and turn from my suitcase, propping my hands on my hips and blowing a strand of hair out of my face. Wyatt smirks as he pushes his blue Henley up his forearms, revealing the ink on his arm, and my lady bits quiver.

They fucking *quiver.*

"All I'm saying is," he continues, but then stops when I keep staring at his arm. "Hey, my eyes are up here."

"That's what she said." I look up at him and smile. "I have a thing for your ink. I don't know what it is. I've seen other men with tattoos before, but I didn't want to nibble on them quite the way I do with yours."

"Well, that's handy," he says and smiles at me in that way he does when he's particularly amused with me. "May I finish?"

"By all means."

"We're only going to be gone for three days. You're not even taking your camera."

"I know. I filmed two videos ahead of time this week, and Nat came over, and we did a bunch of photos for social media, so I have plenty to post. I'm ahead of the game. I just need my phone and my laptop. Nate assures me that the Wi-Fi is good, so I'm ready."

"So why do you need ten outfits?"

"Because I'm a woman and I don't know what the temperature will be at the beach. A girl needs options, Wyatt. Don't you know this by now?"

He shakes his head and laughs softly.

"I don't think this is a high-glam weekend. Not that I don't love it when you get dolled up."

"Really?" I smile and lean in to kiss his muscular shoulder. "That's sweet."

"Haven't you figured it out? I love every look you have, and you have many."

Could he be any sweeter?

"If you keep saying things like that, we'll be late," I reply and turn back to keep throwing things into my suitcase. Actually, *throwing* is the wrong word. I have a system, with packing cubes and lists.

It feeds my organized soul.

"Did I tell you that the pool will be open when we get back?" I ask and do a little booty shake in excitement.

"About six times since we woke up," he replies with a laugh. "You love that pool."

"I know it seems silly, but I really do. I like to work outside when I can, and it's just so peaceful out there with the trees and privacy."

"It's a great outdoor space," he agrees. "You don't have a pool in L.A.?"

"My building does, but it's not private, and it's not nearly this nice. Besides, it's usually too hot to sit by the pool."

My phone rings, and I frown when I see Jules' name.

"Oh no," I mutter before accepting the call. "Please tell me you don't need to cancel."

"I could, but then I'd be lying, and I don't like to do that," she says, then sighs. "I'm sorry, Lia, Stella came down with a bug, and I don't like leaving her when she's sick. Nate and I are going to have to sit this one out."

"Well, damn."

I toss a pair of panties on the bed and sit on the edge of it dejectedly.

"You and Wyatt should still totally go."

Hope springs. "Are you sure? We can plan it for another time."

"No, I mean it. Nate's minions already stocked the place with groceries and the linens are fresh. Even the gazebo has been cleaned, and the cushions replaced this year. It's beautiful, and if you don't go, it'll go to waste."

"That might be a bit dramatic," I reply with a smile. "But I won't say no."

"Good. I'll text you the code to the front door. Enjoy it. And if you have any issues, just call, and Nate will take care of it right away."

"Nate sure is handy."

"Girl, you have *no* idea." She laughs and then groans. "Shit, Stella just threw up in her bed. If anyone ever tells you that being a parent is always glamorous, they're lying. Love you. Have fun. I'm totally jealous."

"Thanks again, and I hope she feels better."

I end the call and glance up to find Wyatt leaning his shoulder on the wall, his hands tucked into his pockets, watching me.

"We're going alone," I say. "Stella's sick."

"And they're okay with us still going?"

"Jules insisted." I stand and continue packing. "And, frankly, I don't want to say no. I've been to Nate's place once before, and it's *so nice*. Are you still up for it?"

"A chance to get you alone at the beach for three days? Hell, yes, I'm still up for it. And just so you know, you'll need way less clothes now that it's just the two of us."

I laugh, but when I look back at him and see the lust in his eyes, I know he's not kidding.

I can't fucking wait.

THE MCKENNA BEACH house is beautiful. A blue, two-story home with a wrap-around porch and tall evergreen trees surrounding it. It's both elegant and comfortable.

The front door is wide, pine, and has a beach scene etched into the oval glass.

"Wow, I was expecting something more—"

"Rustic?" I ask with a smile as I help Wyatt pull our bags out of the back of his Lexus. "I know. But this is way better than a rustic cabin. Come on, I'll show you."

Someone decorated the space in subtle beachy tones, blues and greys in the furniture and rugs. There's an enormous rock fireplace in the middle of the living area.

Jules hung photos from their wedding and baby photos of Stella on the walls. They're in black and white, and immediately draw my eye.

"Let's take our bags upstairs, and then I want to go down to the beach," I say, and Wyatt nods, still looking around.

We choose a bedroom that faces the ocean but isn't the master. Once our toiletries are unpacked, we make our way downstairs.

"This kitchen is amazing." I run my hand over the black granite, enjoying the brightness of the white cabinets, and the huge French doors that lead out to the backside of the wrap-around porch.

"The ocean is churning today," Wyatt says, standing at the doors, his hands on his hips as he watches the waves below. "And we're up awfully high."

"I know, there's a staircase down to the beach," I reply as I open the fridge and take stock of our supplies. "Man, Jules was right. Nate had the place stocked well."

"Excellent. We won't have to leave." Wyatt walks to me and circles his arms around my waist, burying his face in my neck. "I have you all to myself."

"You have me all to yourself when we're at home," I remind him.

"Not the same," he says, his lips moving deliciously over my skin. "Family could show up any minute. Work interrupts. It's always something."

"I'm excited, too," I reply and turn in his arms, hugging him tightly. "And I'm ready for a long walk on the beach, Mr. Crawford."

"Well, then lead the way, Miss Montgomery."

I take his hand in mine and lead him out of the house and down the long staircase. We stop at the gazebo.

"This is great," he says. "We'll use the firepit later."

"We even have the makings for s'mores," I reply with a grin. "And all of these cushions are brand new. I'll be out here a lot."

I continue down to the sand and grin at the roar of the waves, the smell of salt in the air, and the cool breeze hitting my cheeks.

"It's always cool on the Washington coast."

"Mm," I reply with a nod. "Hard to believe this is the same ocean as the one in southern California. Honestly, I prefer this."

"Why?"

"Fewer people. The water is more passionate. Moody." I shrug. "I think it's beautiful."

He kisses my hand, and we walk down to where the sand is wet and packed, making it easier to walk. After about five minutes, I take off my shoes and leave them in the sand, planning to retrieve them on the way back.

"Good idea," Wyatt says, joining me.

"So, I have some really good news," I begin. He looks down at me with raised eyebrows, curiosity all over his face.

"Tell me."

Why am I suddenly so nervous?

"I've been thinking quite a bit since I've been home that maybe I'd like to stay here. Permanently."

His hand tightens on mine, but he stays quiet, which is good because I need to get this out.

"I think it really hit home for me when my dad was in the hospital. Not only do I miss the good things in L.A., like babies being born, and engagement parties, and weddings, but I'm also far away when the bad things happen. What if he'd died and I wasn't able to get here right away?"

He nods, listening intently.

"I love my family, Wyatt. They're fun and they may be quirky, but they always have my back, no matter what."

"You have a great family," he agrees.

"And I have you," I continue. "I am *not* trying to put any kind of pressure on our relationship at all, but the fact remains that I have you, and I don't want to live a three-hour flight away from you. I want to be close to you."

"I'm definitely on the same page there, sweetheart."

I grin. "So, I spoke with Natalie and Luke, and they've agreed to rent the house to me until I find a more permanent place. I also needed to speak with my brand sponsors in L.A. to make sure that they'd help me make the commute work, and they're on board."

He stops walking and turns me to face him.

"Are you telling me that this is for sure? That you're not just throwing it out there?"

There's so much hope in his eyes, it almost buckles my knees in relief.

"I'm for sure relocating to Seattle," I confirm, and am swept up in his arms. He spins us around twice and then begins kissing the hell out of me, just as the sky decides to open up and dump on us.

Wyatt doesn't seem to give a shit.

He's cupping my face, his thumbs brushing over my cheeks as he kisses me, nibbles my lips, tickles the corners of my mouth.

"Wyatt," I murmur as the water sluices over our bodies. "Raining."

He just picks me up and walks back toward the house with me in his arms. My legs are wrapped around his waist, my arms around his neck, and he's supporting my ass effortlessly. The rain is warm.

I tip my forehead against his so I can catch my breath.

"I guess you're okay with my plan."

"So fucking okay with it," he agrees and begins to climb the stairs.

"We're barefoot."

"I don't care."

When we reach the gazebo, he sets me on my feet and turns to start the fire. I immediately strip my shirt over my head and let it fall to the floor with a soggy *thud*. The rest of my clothes follow, and when he turns back to me, I'm sitting back on the cushions, completely naked.

"You didn't like those clothes?"

"They're wet." I grin and spread my legs wide, knowing he can see the most intimate part of me, and let my fingers softly drag over my skin toward my center. I bite my lip, watching Wyatt's eyes as they follow my hand, and when I begin to make circles over my clit, he swears a blue streak as he strips out of his clothes.

"You're so fucking sexy," he says and joins me, laying me back over the cushions and cupping my breasts in his hands, flicking my nipples with his thumbs. "Everything you do sets my body on fire."

"Everything?"

"Every fucking thing," he confirms before sucking one nipple firmly into his mouth, then letting it go with a *pop*. "I'm permanently hard for you, Amelia."

"That's fine with me," I reply and reach down to try to cup his cock in my hand, but he's too far away. "I can't reach you."

"I'm going to take you, right out here in the open," he says, ignoring me. "It's going to be hard and fast."

"Hell, yes," I reply, already soaked for him. He pins my hands over my head and thrusts inside me, making me gasp as my body stretches and accommodates him. "Fuck."

"That's right, baby." He bites my neck, then licks the tender spot before traveling to my shoulder. "Jesus, I can't get enough of you."

"Good." I strain against his hands, but he holds firm. "I want to touch you."

"I didn't ask you," he replies and pins me in a hot, controlling gaze that only makes me wetter. "You're mine, do you understand me?"

I blink rapidly, surprised by the sudden intensity in him, and nod, completely under his spell. "I'm yours."

He pulls out and flips me over. I don't even have time to feel self-conscious before he straddles my thighs, pushing my cheeks together. His thumbs dive into my folds, spreading my wetness, and my pussy to accommodate his cock.

"Holy shit," I mutter when he pushes inside me. "God, that feels different."

"Are you okay?" he asks, and I fall in love with him all over again. He may be taking me, but he's careful to make sure I feel safe.

"So damn good," I confirm. "Feels so good."

The tip of his cock pushes slightly against the deepest part of me, and with my legs and ass pressed closed, I feel more full than I ever have in my life.

I think I just found my new favorite position.

He brushes his thumb over my asshole, and I come apart, pulsing against him and crying out as the intense orgasm rolls through me.

"Jesus, Amelia," he groans as he comes inside me.

Before I can catch my breath, he pulls me off the cushions and into his arms. He flips a switch, turning the fire off, and carries me up the stairs.

"Where are we going now?"

"To the shower. I need to wash you and bury myself inside you again."

"You took my news well."

He smiles down at me. "I'm a very happy man."

IT TURNS OUT that Wyatt was right. I brought way too many clothes.

Since our walk on the beach two days ago, I've hardly had clothes on my body. We've been in bed, making love, eating, watching the water.

Yes, he's quite happy with my decision to move, and that only cements for me that it's the right decision.

I woke early this morning, and couldn't resist pulling on some clothes, grabbing a cup of coffee, and coming down to the gazebo to watch the world wake up. Whales were breaching when I first arrived, but I haven't seen any in a while.

I can't believe how different my life is, even from just a year ago. Vinnie was still harassing me, trying to tie the divorce up in court.

I guess that latter part is still happening, but I have a feeling we're almost finished with that. Even if I have to pay him more money, he'll be gone for good soon.

I thought I was happy in L.A., running a social media empire, attending fashion shows and influencer parties. Not that those things aren't fun. They're a blast. But it's also nothing at all compared to what I have in Seattle.

And I haven't lost that. I'll be in L.A. monthly to work on my make-up brand and attend many of those things. I can't believe it's real, but it looks like I'm going to have the best of both worlds, and to say that I'm a bit giddy is an understatement.

I don't remember the last time I felt this happy. Lighthearted. Like the weight of the world *wasn't* draped over my shoulders, making me feel as if I were being pounded into the earth.

All I've ever wanted is to follow my passion and be supported in that. Vinnie hated everything about what I did. *Hated.* He mocked me and made me feel small. He hurt me.

And now, I feel as if I can do *anything* because Wyatt is happy to encourage and support me. He rejoices in my success with me. He's my rock.

My phone pings with a text, and I smile at Wyatt's name.

I lost you.

All of this is because of him. This happiness. This contentedness. This *freedom.* Ironic, isn't it, that being in a relationship with someone wonderful is freeing?

On the gazebo with my coffee. Didn't want to wake you.

I didn't know that I was so empty inside in L.A. That I was missing something. Not that I'm not a whole person by myself. I am. I'm not one of those people who think I need someone else to complete me.

But Wyatt complements me beautifully. Where I'm a dreamer, he's a thinker. Where I'm silly, he's grounded.

And the love he shows me is unlike anything I've ever known. There are no strings. No expectations.

Just love.

"Hey, beautiful," he says as he joins me, carrying his own mug of coffee and a small carafe. "I brought more so you wouldn't have to go up for it."

This, right here, is what I'm talking about. He's thoughtful and kind.

He owns my heart.

fifteen

Wyatt

"That's what I have for you today, friends. I hope this tutorial helped you with how to use your highlighters and bronzers. I'll link the products I used today below, and be sure to comment to let me know what some of your favorite products are. I'll see you next week, but in the meantime, remember, you're already beautiful, just the way you are. Have a great week, everyone."

She clicks a button, and the recording stops. Without missing a beat, she immediately goes back to the beginning of the video to scrutinize herself.

She's fucking amazing to watch when she's working.

"I brought you something," I say, catching her attention. Her blue eyes light up when she looks up at me, and I want to scoop her up and take her to the bedroom.

Do not pass go, do not collect the two hundred dollars.

"We had a deal," she says, pointing her manicured finger at me.

"What deal was that?" My voice is full of innocent bafflement, even though I know damn well what deal it was.

"No hanky-panky while we're both trying to work," she says, taking the plate of fruit and yogurt away from me. "You're looking at me with the look."

"The look?"

"The sexy look," she clarifies. She pops a blueberry into her mouth.

"There's no time for you and your sexy looks."

I smirk and watch as she pops a strawberry into her mouth and chews happily.

"I didn't even know I was hungry."

"That's what I'm here for," I remind her, then lean down to lightly kiss her. "How much more work do you have here?"

"At least a couple of hours," she replies, blowing a breath through her lips. "I'm sorry. You don't have to stay if you're bored."

"I have plenty of my own work." I kiss the top of her head and glance down at the screen where she's already started editing the video. "You look amazing on camera."

"Thanks." She smiles and takes a bite of yogurt. "It's the lights."

"It's the woman." I kiss her head again, breathing in the fresh scent of her. "I'll be in the other room if you need anything."

"Thanks." She doesn't even glance up when I leave the room, already engrossed in her work.

She looks fierce, sitting there with her hair down, her makeup flawless, and that little frown between her eyebrows as she scrutinizes every second of the video, making sure it's just so.

Her work ethic is admirable.

There are many reasons to love her. I'm completely enamored with her.

When she told me last weekend at the beach house that she'd decided to move to Seattle, I felt like I won the fucking lottery. I knew that I'd never be able to say goodbye to her when the time came. Long distance relationships just don't work.

At least, I've never known anyone to make it work.

And I want this to work.

Now, I don't have to go through the agony of knowing she's far away, wondering what she's doing, missing her. I want us to be a part of each other's lives, every day.

While she's been in her office, I've made myself a makeshift work area in the dining room. I have my laptop, iPad, and paper, not to mention, plenty of coffee. I could easily go home to work, but it's been nice knowing that she's just right upstairs.

I can hear her voice, and it doesn't interrupt my flow in the least. It soothes me in a way I never expected.

Before I can dive back into the task at hand, my phone rings.

"Hey, Levi."

"Am I interrupting?"

"Nope. What's up?"

"I might have mentioned to Mom that Jace and I are coming to your place on Sunday, and she invited herself."

"That's fine." I lean back in the chair and scratch my cheek. "There will be plenty of food."

"I just felt bad. I mean, how do I tell her she's not invited without hurting her feelings?"

"It's fine," I repeat and smile when I hear Amelia talking to herself. "She has to meet the parents sooner or later, right?"

"If you're willing to let her meet Mom, you're smitten."

"I am," I confirm.

"Do you need us to bring anything?"

"No, it's going to be casual. And Amelia invited her brother and sister, as well."

"I'm sorry, am I talking to Wyatt? My brother? The one who's been commitmentphobic for a few years and *never* would have hosted a party like this at his house?"

"Ha ha, smartass. I've hosted parties."

"Not grown-up parties, with families and stuff."

I laugh. "I'm all grown up now, big brother. I'll see you on Sunday."

"NOW YOU NEED *me* to take care of *you*."

I glance up at the sound of her voice to find her standing at the foot of the stairs, watching me with a soft smile on her stunning face.

"Is that so?"

She nods and walks into the kitchen. She reaches into the fridge for two bottles of water and brings me one, then surprises me by climbing into my lap and wrapping her arms around my neck.

"I don't want to get into trouble," I murmur before she plants her full lips on mine. I sink into the kiss, losing myself in her, the way I always do where Amelia's concerned. She plunges her fingers into my hair and makes a fist, holding on tightly.

I can't stop my hands from roaming over her tight body any more than I can control the tides. I cup her cheek, then let my hand fall to her breast, worrying the nipple into a tight bud under her thin tank.

"Mm," she murmurs, grinning against my mouth, and I let my hand travel farther south, under the hem of her denim shorts and panties until I find her already wet center with my fingertips. "Fuck."

"You like that?" I ask against her lips. She nods and holds onto me tighter as I rub light circles around her hard clit, reveling in how her entire body tenses under my touch.

"What's not to like?" Her voice is husky, she's panting, and she's squirming in my lap. "Fill me, babe."

"No." I raise a brow when she frowns at me and continue to wreak havoc on the most sensitive part of her delectable body. "I'm in control here, sweetheart. That's right, I want you to feel this."

"Can't do anything else," she says and squeezes her eyes shut. I push a finger inside her, and she cries out and convulses around me, coming against my hand.

I pull my hand out of her pants and lick my finger clean, loving the taste and smell of her. She's the most powerful aphrodisiac there is.

"Are you going to fuck me now?" she asks.

"No." Her eyes spring open in surprise. "I don't want to get sent home. You'd better get off my lap."

She looks taken aback and then starts to laugh in the husky way she does that sets every nerve ending on end. "You're such a smartass."

"I like to keep you wanting more," I reply and kiss her neck before setting her on her feet. She reaches down and cups my cock through my jeans.

"Likewise," she says, then winks and walks away, her hips swaying as she moves across the room and back up the stairs.

I push my hands through my hair and call myself an idiot.

I'm the one who has to sit here with a hard-on like a sixteen-year-old on a first date.

HEY, BABE, I'M gonna be a few mins late. I'm sorry!

I grin and text Amelia back. *No problem. We'll be here.*

"You have a beautiful home," Amelia's father says, and my mother immediately jumps in with tales of my last house and why this one is so much better.

With Mom around, I'll never have to speak again.

Levi winks at me and passes me a beer. Everyone is here, my brothers, Amelia's siblings, and our parents.

And so far, everyone is getting along well.

Not that I thought they wouldn't.

Jace, Anastasia, and Archer are standing on the edge of the patio, looking out at the Sound and laughing at something Anastasia said.

Amelia rushes outside, panting, and looking as beautiful as I've ever seen her with her hair pulled up, minimal makeup on, and a casual black T-shirt with shorts.

"Hey, guys, sorry I'm late—" She stops in mid-sentence and stares at our parents, then at me, and plasters a big, fake smile on her gorgeous face. "Hey, everybody. This is a surprise."

"It's so lovely to finally meet you," my mom says as she and Dad stand, and Mom immediately folds Amelia into a hug. "I've heard so much about you, dear."

Amelia looks shell-shocked as my dad also pulls her in for a hug.

"Lia, these affectionate people are clearly my parents, Linus and Melody."

"So nice to meet you," she says with a nod and then looks over at her own parents. "Hi, Mom and Daddy. Have you all met each other already?"

"Oh, yes," my mom says happily. "We've become fast friends. Sherri and I both love to knit, and we were just talking about our favorite yarn shops."

"How nice," Amelia says, that fake smile still on her lips as she looks up at me. "Wyatt? Can I talk to you for just a second?"

"Of course." I follow her inside, through the house to my office, where we're as far away from the party as we can get.

"What the hell?"

"To be fair, I didn't know that your parents were coming either," I say, putting my hands up in surrender. "They came with Anastasia."

"But you *did* know about your parents?" she asks, her voice a tiny bit shrill.

Or a lot shrill.

"I forgot to tell you."

"How could you forget?"

"You sat your sexy ass in my lap, and I had my fingers buried inside you," I remind her, bringing color to her cheeks. "So, yeah, I forgot."

She blows out a breath and hangs her head, and I immediately pull her into my arms, hugging her close.

"This is okay," I say firmly. "Our parents were going to meet each other eventually."

"I just wasn't mentally prepared for it to be today," she mumbles against my chest. "I'm not dressed for it. My hair is a mess. I thought we were just having a casual cookout with our siblings."

"We are," I reply and laugh when she stares up at me as if I've just told her the world is flat. "Really, we are. You look fantastic. It's just our families."

"Pshaw. Right. It's just the *first time* that I'm meeting your parents, and I want it to be perfect. You only get one chance to make a first impression, Wyatt."

"I honestly don't think you have anything to be worried about," I reply and kiss her forehead, then her lips. "Let's go out there and just have fun. They love us. This isn't a big deal."

"You're lucky I love *you*," she says and slaps my arm, making me scowl. "You need to tell me these things, Crawford."

"You're such a stickler," I reply, rubbing my arm. "A violent stickler at that."

She smirks and leads me back outside, and we spend the next hour cooking steaks on the grill, talking and laughing.

Well, most of us do. Amelia is still tense and has suddenly turned into a formal hostess, constantly asking if she can freshen up everyone's drinks like it's her job.

"I'd love some more tea, darling," Sherri says when Amelia asks, and this time when Lia takes the glass and walks inside, I follow her into the kitchen.

"Enough," I say firmly and pin her against the countertop, my hands planted on either side of her hips, and my face inches from hers.

"Enough what?"

"Enough of this. I don't know what's gotten into you, but this isn't a reception full of strangers. It's our family, and they're having a good time. If they want drinks, they know damn well where to find the fucking kitchen."

"It's kind of a big deal," she says, shaking her head. "Our whole families are meeting for the first time."

"They haven't come to fisticuffs yet," I remind her and then smile when she narrows her eyes on me. "Seriously, you're worrying for nothing."

At that moment, we can hear laughter coming from outside, driving my point home.

"See?"

"I'm just all nervous," she admits and rolls her shoulders. "I want your parents to like me."

"They like you." I lean in and kiss her neck, and she pulls away, making me frown.

"They could walk in any second."

"I don't give a fuck." I kiss her neck again, and she doesn't pull away this time. "This is my house, and I'm kissing the woman I love in it. I don't have to explain myself to them."

She melts against me as my mouth explores hers. My hands drift up under her shirt, and my fingertips glide gently over her ribcage, making her shiver.

"Are you loosening up yet?" I ask against her neck, and she squeezes my ass in response. "Kinky."

She giggles. "I'm not kinky."

I raise a brow. "No? What if I tied you to my bed and ate you out until you were a sweaty, quivering mess."

"Well, I mean, I wouldn't say no."

"Are you starting to feel better?"

"No, now I'm just turned on."

"That's better than anxious," I reply and kiss her softly before pulling away. "Now, let's go back out there before my brothers accuse me of fucking you in the kitchen."

She looks horrified for a moment and then breaks out into laughter, which doesn't help the state of my cock in the least.

Out back, Archer and Jace have just set up the cornhole game that Archer brought with him.

"You brought it," Amelia says, excited. "Are you ready to have your ass handed to you?"

She covers her mouth in surprise and looks over at my parents who just laugh.

"Honey, cursing isn't the end of the world," my dad says. "Go flip them all some shit."

She grins. "I like you."

Dad winks at her, and we spend the next hour tossing small bean bags across my lawn, aiming for the hole in the middle of a board.

"That's right, I knocked you out, sucker," Amelia calls to her brother and then sticks her tongue out at him.

"I had no idea you were so passionate about cornhole," I say with a laugh.

"Oh, I'm very good at this game," she replies happily. Since our moment in the kitchen, she's much more relaxed. "I can kick Archer's ass."

"In your dreams, little girl," he taunts back. "You got lucky."

"So lucky that I've beaten you eight games in a row?" she asks and does a little dance. The Macarena, if I'm not mistaken.

"You cheat," Anastasia says.

"You can't cheat at cornhole," Amelia insists. "You're all just bad losers. And I'm the victor!"

She thrusts her fists into the air and jogs around the yard in victory, making me laugh. I love this playful side of her.

She stops in front of me, offering her lips up in celebration. I immediately kiss her chastely, and then she rubs her hands together.

"What's for dessert?"

sixteen

Amelia

I'm either having an excellent, sexy dream, or Wyatt is waking me up with his tongue.

God bless him.

He's so fucking good at this wake-up sex thing. His hands are gentle but sensual. His mouth is smooth and confident. And his sexy, warm body is naked and hovering over me.

I'm on my tummy. My first instinct is to flip over because there's light filtering through the gauzy curtains, but then I remember, this is Wyatt, and he loves my ass.

Cellulite and all.

"Don't you even think about trying to flip over," he murmurs, not lifting his lips from my spine.

"Are you a mind reader?"

He smiles against me, then licks all the way up to my neck, sending shivers rolling over my body.

"I know you," he whispers against my ear. His nakedness is pressed against me now, and his cock is *hard*.

"It seems you do."

He nibbles on the ball of my shoulder. "You're delicious in the morning, sweetheart."

"You're good at the morning sex."

"I can't resist you when you're in my bed, gorgeous. Naked. God, you're every dream I've ever had."

I glance back at him over my shoulder. "You say some sweet things, but you don't have to butter me up. I'm all for some morning sex."

He grins. "I'm not buttering you up for anything."

He flips me over and settles his pelvis against mine, rocking back and forth. My eyes are going to cross and roll back in my head.

"You like that?"

"Good Lord, yes," I reply and reach up to brush his hair off his brow. "I haven't found anything that you do that I don't like."

"Excellent." He lowers himself so he can press his lips to mine, and I wrap my arms and legs around him, holding on tightly as he pushes inside of me, still rocking gently. "You're always so wet. So ready for me."

"Well, you've got the foreplay thing down." I grin as his eyes narrow, and he starts to move faster, just a bit harder. "And you're visually stunning."

"Is that so?"

"Oh, yeah." I sigh and close my eyes, enjoying the way his body rocks mine, and how fully he fills me. "All of this is damn good."

He chuckles and links his fingers through mine, pinning our hands to the bed beside my head. The lovemaking is slow and hot, with deep breaths and gasps, sweaty bodies and sighs.

I never want it to end.

But before I know it, I can feel the orgasm building, and as if he can sense it, he presses his thumb against my clit, and that's all I need to fall apart. Spectacularly.

"So beautiful," he whispers as he's coming down from his own orgasm. He kisses my cheek, my nose, my forehead. "You make me fucking crazy, Amelia."

"Back at you, sexy man."

He plants a firm kiss on my lips, then climbs off the bed.

"I have to take a shower."

"Okay."

He grins and, suddenly, reaches down to pull me off of the bed and into his arms, marching to the bathroom.

"I guess I need a shower, too?"

"I dirtied you up. I need to clean up my mess."

I giggle as he sets me down and starts the water. He reaches for a bag sitting on the countertop and pulls out a shower puff, the shower gel I use, and my favorite kind of razor.

"Wow."

"Now you don't have to run home all of the time to shower," he says and winks at me. "And I can have my way with you in the water."

He pulls me into his spacious, tiled stand-up shower. The glass door is heavy and already steaming up. There's a bench on one wall, where he has a bottle of shampoo and conditioner waiting for me.

"You thought of everything," I say as he lathers up my shower puff and begins cleaning my skin. "I like a man who's prepared."

"I'm *very* prepared," he says, his face serious, but I know he's being silly, and this is a side of him that I *love*. "I make lists all of the time."

"Really. Lists. That *is* impressive."

"I know. Also, I've never been late paying a bill. Because I set reminders on my phone."

"Now you're just trying to get back in my pants."

I giggle when he slaps my wet ass, then turns me away from him so he can wash my back.

"You're not wearing any pants," he reminds me. "So, I'm already kind of in them."

"True." He lets the puff fall to the tile and grips my hips, pulling me to him.

"Bend over and grab that bench, baby."

I look over my shoulder with a raised brow. The humor has left his hazel eyes, replaced by pure, unadulterated lust.

"It wasn't a question," he says, and I bite my lip, complying. He's quickly inside me again, but it's not light and fun this time. It's hard and fast and over quickly, with both of us quivering and panting. He spins me back into his arms and hugs me close.

"The bossiness is sexy," I inform him, catching my breath. "But if you think you'll get away with it outside of the bedroom, you can think again."

He smirks. "I love you, Amelia. You make me laugh more than I have in years." He reaches for the puff and lathers it up again, then gets back to work. "What are your plans today?"

"Work." I sigh as he grazes my shoulders. It feels fantastic. "You?"

"I'll be working downtown all day," he says. "So I won't see you until later tonight."

"Okay." He rinses me off, and I take the puff from him, returning the favor. "I'd better get you all clean now."

"Yes, you did make a mess, didn't you?"

"Oh, yeah, and I'll do it again later."

"Good girl."

IT'S SEVERAL HOURS later when the doorbell rings. A postal carrier has me sign for a letter.

It's from my attorney. Vinnie has finally been served, and we have a mediation date. My heart speeds up as I skim down the letter.

I have to be in mediation in ten days.

Ten days!

I immediately reach for my phone and call Pam.

"Hi, Pam, I just got your letter."

"Do you have any issues with getting here in time for the meeting?" she asks.

"No, I'll absolutely be there. But is there a way for us not to have to be in the same room? Like, can the mediator just go back and forth between two conference rooms so I don't have to be near him?"

"Sure, we can do that. There will be an extra charge for the second conference room."

Of course, there will be. I roll my eyes, not even wanting to think about the tens of thousands I've already paid Pam in legal fees.

"That's fine, I'd rather not have to see him."

"I understand. We'll meet here in my office. Vinnie and his lawyer will be here as well, in a different room, and a mediator will be here to hopefully get this all settled."

"If we can come to an agreement on that day, how long will it be until the divorce is final?"

"Fourteen days," she says, and I immediately break out into a happy dance. "Let me know if you need anything, but otherwise, I'll see you in ten days."

"Thanks, Pam."

I hang up and do a little shimmy. This will be *perfect*. Maybe Wyatt can fly down with me, and we can work on packing up my condo and get my car, then drive back to Seattle. Road trips are fun, and we'd have a great time. He may not be able to take time off of work, but I hope he can.

God, I'm just so *excited*. By this time next month, I'll finally be rid of Vinnie forever and I can move on with my life. It's about damn time.

I'm still holding my phone, and it starts to ring in my hand, startling me.

"Hi, Stasia. What's up?"

"I need your help," she says. "It's not an emergency, but I had two orders come in for this weekend. I committed to both and then realized that I only have two hands. Can you come help me bake the cakes while I decorate? I know it's last minute, but I could use your hands."

"I have excellent hands," I agree and laugh when she snorts on the other end. "I can totally help. I'll bring food, too."

"You're seriously bailing me out," she says. "See you soon?"

"Yep, I'll be there within the hour."

I hang up and immediately text Wyatt.

Hey, I gotta go help my sister. I've been roped into cake duty. Probably won't be home until late.

I run upstairs to change clothes, and as I'm climbing into Jules' car to head to Bellevue, Wyatt replies.

Have fun. Love you.

I grin and reply with a *love you too* and head toward Anastasia's shop. Life's damn good. I'm ridiculously in love, and all of the legal shit is about to be over.

It just doesn't get better than this.

"HOLY FUCK, WE baked a lot of cake today." We're sitting in Anastasia's apartment, drinking a bottle of wine, stuffed full of takeout pizza.

"So much cake," I agree and take another sip of wine. I don't drink often, so it's already going to my head. "You should bring on some help, especially if you're getting this much work. You can't do it all yourself."

"I know, and I'm looking around. I wasn't expecting to have to expand so soon." She grins and leans over to clink her glass to mine. "Here's to successful businesses, for both of us."

"We fucking kick ass," I reply with a nod. "Of course, I learned it all from you."

"You've had too much to drink already," she says, rolling her eyes.

"No, I haven't. You have such a strong work ethic, Stasia. You always have. And I admit that I've just always wanted to make you proud of me. So I work hard, like you. Because I do."

My nose itches. Maybe I have had a little much to drink.

"See? Too much to drink."

"Doesn't make it any less true." I shrug a shoulder. "Are you doing okay? With the new business and moving back here and all of it?"

"I'm happy," she says with a nod. "It's good to be home."

"I know." I clear my throat. "I'm moving home, too."

"What? When?"

"In a few weeks." I smile and tell her about going back down for mediation and packing up my things while I'm there. "I'm so excited. I want to be close to you guys."

"What does Wyatt think?"

"He's excited. Relieved, I think."

"I get it," she says with a nod. "Things are serious there."

"Yeah." I scratch my nose again. "He's so hot, sis. Like, steaming hot."

"He's definitely hot." She laughs. "I think I'm a little tipsy, too."

"We haven't done this in *years*." I giggle and pour more wine into our glasses. "It's okay that you think Wyatt's hot. Because he is."

"Vinnie wasn't hot," she says with a scowl. "I guess someone might think he is, but he's such a douchetard that he's *not*."

"Agreed." We clink glasses again. "I miss Wyatt. I'm going to text him."

"Good idea. Make him send you pictures."

I nod and open my phone.

Hey, bbe. Luv u. Send me a dick pic, k?

I giggle and set my phone aside. "I totally just asked him for a dick pic."

"I didn't say that," she says and dissolves into giggles. "That's kind of pervy."

"He has a stellar dick," I reply as my phone pings.

Not happening, even for you. Are you drunk?

"He asked if I'm drunk."

We stare at each other and then dissolve into more laughter.

"My fingers don't work well, so I'm just gonna call him."

"Good idea."

The phone only rings once when he picks up.

"Are you okay?" he asks.

"Oh, yeah. I'm fantastic. Hi."

"Hi, baby." I can hear the smile in his voice, and it makes me gooey. "You're sexy."

"Thank you. So, on a scale of one to ten, how drunk are you?"

"Oh, I'm like a seven." I hiccup and then scratch my nose again. The fucker is so itchy! "I don't think I should come home tonight."

"She'll stay with me," Anastasia yells out.

"Good plan," Wyatt says.

"I miss your penis," I inform him, and Stasia snorts loudly. "Like, you should send me a picture."

"No way," he says and laughs. "You can see it tomorrow."

"So far away," I reply with a sigh. "I didn't realize you were mean."

"Damn, you're wasted. Get some sleep, baby."

"He calls me baby," I inform Anastasia, who's just watching me with a sleepy smile. "Okay, see you tomorrow. Love you and your penis."

I hang up and toss my phone on the ottoman.

"He's good for you," she says.

"Yeah. I think I'm good for him, too."

"I think so." She yawns. "We should go to bed. I'm so tired."

"Where am I sleeping?"

She blinks in surprise and then shrugs one shoulder. "Looks like you're bunking with me."

"We used to do that a lot as kids, remember?"

"You're a bed hog," she says as she leads me into her bedroom. She tosses me a clean T-shirt, and we change, then climb into her king-sized bed and snuggle down. I scooch over and hug her from behind. "Jesus, I forgot how much you like to snuggle. Get off of me."

"I need to snuggle." Yeah, I sound whiny. I don't care. "I have to be able to sleep."

"You can sleep without having your cold feet and hands all over me." She laughs and shoves me away. "Go away."

"No." I hold onto her tightly. "I'm gonna make you snuggle me. I'm your baby sister, and I need you."

"You're a pain in my ass."

"Love you, sissy."

"Love you, too."

MY CAR WON'T fucking start.

Strike that. *Jules'* car won't start. I'm staring at it as if it's betrayed me and sigh heavily. I'm hungover so badly, I can barely see. Anastasia has more work today, so she can't run me home.

So, I call my knight in shining armor.

"Good morning," he says, and I pull the phone away from my head, scowling at it.

"There's no need to yell, Wyatt."

He laughs, and I scowl deeper.

"What's up, sweetheart?"

"Jules' car won't start. Can you please come get me?"

"Of course." I can hear commotion on his end. "Just text me the address."

"Can't you be psychic just this once so I don't have to actually move?"

"You must be in rough shape this morning," he says with a chuckle.

"Unfortunately, I'm not psychic."

"Okay, I'll send it. Please hurry."

"I'm on my way."

seventeen

Wyatt

I hated being away from her last night. I could have offered to go get her, but it sounded like she was having fun with her sister, and they don't do that often enough. So instead, I missed her, worked myself into a coma, and couldn't get out of the house fast enough to go rescue her this morning.

I've begun to wonder if having her permanently across the street is enough. What the fuck am I saying? Of course, it's not enough. And some might say that it's too soon for this, but I want her to live with me. I want her things mixed with mine. She's already all over my home. Her scent is on my bed sheets. Her stuff in my shower.

I can't be there without seeing her everywhere.

It just makes sense to ask her to move in. If she's not ready, I can be a patient man until she is, but I hope it doesn't take long.

I want her. Always.

The GPS guides me to Anastasia's building in Bellevue, and there's Amelia, waiting for me. She looks a bit grouchy. Her hair isn't brushed, and it's down around her face. She looks small, her arms crossed over her chest.

Frankly, she looks miserable.

"Hey," she says as she climbs into my car and braces her head in her hand. "You're breathing really loudly."

I chuckle and reach around her to pull her seatbelt over her, then kiss her temple gently.

"Did you take anything?" I ask softly.

"Yeah, just now. It should kick in soon."

I pull out of the parking lot, headed for the I-90 toward Seattle.

"It sounded like you had fun."

"We did," she says. "But Stasia wouldn't snuggle me, the bitch. She's never been much of a snuggler."

She smacks her lips. "Why does wine always do this? My mouth is dry. And I forgot my damn sunglasses in Jules' car."

I take off my glasses and pass them to her. She glances up in surprise. "You need them more than me right now. Here."

"Thanks." She slips them on, and they slip down her nose just a bit, making me smile. "Your head is bigger than mine."

"I have water for you, too." I snap the top off and pass it to her.

"And there you go, taking care of me again," she murmurs. She opens her purse, then sighs and tips back her head.

"What's wrong?"

"Do you want the list?"

I grin over at her before merging over a lane. "Of course."

"I didn't put my lip balm in my purse."

"Here." I open the center console and pass her some lip balm.

"You're so sweet," she says softly. "And I'm sorry that I'm too hungover to be properly thankful."

"You're fine," I assure her, patting her thigh. "I'm sorry that you're miserable."

"I should know better," she says and shrugs one shoulder. "Wine always does this. I could drink tequila until the sun comes up and feel fine after. But wine is a bitch, who likes to make me feel like someone's squeezing my head with a vise."

"Sip your water. You're dehydrated."

"Yes, Dr. Crawford."

I wink at her and merge onto the 520, headed toward home.

"We'll get you in a hot shower, and I'll make you something to eat, and you'll feel better."

"If I want to take a nap, will you snuggle me?"

"You don't even have to ask," I assure her. "I'm glad that you and Anastasia had time together. You don't usually do that."

"We used to," she says. "We've always been close. But after I married my ex, we grew apart. Vinnie didn't like my family, and he wasn't a fan of us spending a lot of time together. Which really wasn't a problem because I lived in L.A. and Anastasia lived in San Francisco until recently. I got out of the habit of calling her and confiding in her. It's been really great to get that back."

"I'm sure it has. I've always been pretty close to Levi and Jace, as well. They can be a pain in my ass, and when we were young, they liked to torment me relentlessly. But if anyone else tried to bully me, they were right there, ready to kick ass."

"Exactly," she says, a small smile tickling her lips. "Also, it sucks when your family doesn't love your spouse. It just makes everything uncomfortable, so I got used to staying away. I could blame him for it, but the truth is, I wasn't strong enough to put my foot down and say *no*. This is my family, and I love them."

"I get it," I reply and sigh, feeling my jaw clench. "My family didn't like Claudia either. And sometimes it was easier to do what made her happy because she was the one I lived with."

"Yep, you get it," she says and then clears her throat. "But enough about all of that. I guess I should say now that if you have any issues with my family, you should go ahead and say so. Because I won't compromise my relationship with them for anyone. Ever."

"I like your family." I reach over and take her hand in mine. "And even if I didn't, I'd never ask you to choose between us."

"I like yours, too. It's handy."

I pull into her driveway. "Did you call anyone about the car?"

"I texted Jules. She said Nate was going to have it taken care of."

"Good. Let's get you in the shower."

"I love you, Wyatt. And God knows I want to climb you every time I see you, but I just don't think I can do the sex right now."

I laugh from the bottom of my gut and lean over to kiss her cheek.

"Don't worry, sweetheart, you're safe from my libido for now."

She cups my cheek. "Thanks for rescuing me."

"Anytime."

I follow her upstairs, grinning at how slowly she's taking the stairs. When she walks into the bedroom, I hurry into the bathroom and get the water flowing in the shower. When I return to the bedroom, she's just sitting on the edge of the bed, staring off into space.

"Are you sleep-sitting?" I ask with a raised brow.

"I think so."

"How's your head?"

"I think it's still attached." She reaches up and touches it. "Yep, still there."

"You're so funny." I cross to her and slip her shirt up over her head, throwing it into the hamper. "You have to stand up so I can finish getting you naked."

"I think this is your favorite hobby." She does as I ask and braces her hands on my shoulders as I slip her shorts and panties down her legs, then unfasten her bra and let it fall to the floor.

"It ranks right up there," I agree. "Come on."

I take her hand and lead her to the shower. She steps inside and immediately lets the hot water sluice over her head and down her body. Her nipples harden, and it takes everything in me to not strip down and join her.

"Are you okay here?"

"Yeah, this is nice. My head's starting to feel better, too."

"Good. Do you want breakfast? Maybe some scrambled eggs and toast?"

"I love you," she says, rubbing the water out of her eyes so she can look at me. "I love you a lot. And not just for this but because you're a good person, Wyatt."

"I love you, too." I lean in and kiss her lips. "You get comfortable and come downstairs."

She nods. "This won't take long."

I walk downstairs and through the kitchen out back to the pool, cleaning off her favorite lounge chair, then I spread a soft blanket over it so she can curl up there in the sun for a while after she has her breakfast.

My girl loves the pool.

Once that is set up, I brew her a cup of coffee and take it up to her. She's just walking out of the shower, wrapping her hair in a towel.

"Did you just make me coffee?"

"I did." I hold it out of her grasp and purse my lips, waiting for a kiss.

She grins and obliges, then sighs in happiness after the first sip. "Totally keeping you," she whispers. "I'll be down in five minutes. I'm not going to dry my hair, I'll just twist it up."

"Okay, baby. No hurry."

"No, there is a hurry because I'm starving." She winks, then reaches out and pulls me to her. "But I'm not opposed to the whole sex thing now. I mean, I'm naked and everything."

"And ridiculously tempting," I reply, pressing my lips to hers. I let myself sink into her for just a moment, loving the way her naked skin feels, soft and damp from the shower, and smile against her mouth. "Do you know how badly I want to be inside you right now?"

"I'm right here," she replies, holding onto my shirt at the sides.

"After you eat," I promise and kiss her once more until we're both breathless. "You'll eat eggs, and I'll eat you."

She grins happily. "Promises, promises."

"Don't get sassy, or I'll slap your ass while I'm at it."

"Seriously, stop talking like this unless you're willing to do something about it."

I laugh and walk back down to the kitchen and pull out the pan for the eggs. Bread, eggs, and butter come out of the fridge, and when I turn back around, I notice a letter on the counter with a certified envelope next to it.

. . . in L.A. in ten days of receiving this letter . . .

I frown and move back to the task at hand, not wanting to invade her privacy but now curious about it. I've just opened the bread when Amelia walks into the kitchen, looking much better than she did when I picked her up.

"You look better."

"I feel much better," she says.

"I didn't mean to snoop, but I see that you have to be in L.A. soon?"

She frowns and looks down at the letter, and then her whole face lights up with a bright smile. "Yes. I have to go back for the legal crap I told you about, but I have to talk to you about this."

"Shoot."

"Well, I was hoping that you might be able to take a week off of work so we could fly down together, pack up my place, and get my car. Then we can road trip it back to Seattle."

I nod, thinking about my schedule. "I'm pretty sure I can move some things around. That would be fun."

"I think so, too. I'll hire a mover for most of it, but I'd like to pack up my personal things, and my valuables, and bring them back in the car."

"Makes sense." I smile and then pull her into my arms. "This is really happening."

"So happening," she replies and hugs me tightly. "I'm *so* ready to be out of L.A. I like it there, but I want to be here. Not to mention, I'm beyond excited to have this divorce final and finished."

She pulls out of my arms and paces the kitchen, still talking, but I can't hear anything except *divorce final and finished.*

"Stop." My voice is hard. She pauses and whips her head around.

"What?"

"What did you just say?"

"That it was a technicality and it sucks?"

"Before that." *I didn't even hear that part.*

"That I'm ready for the divorce to be final?"

"Yes, that."

"Oh my God, Wyatt, I'm *so ready* for it to be final. He was such a jerk . . ."

I've been fucking a married woman.

" . . . and I thought it was over. I mean, I left him years ago . . ."

She's not divorced. She said she was divorced.

" . . . party and everything. I mean, how humiliating is that, right? But then . . ."

She's been cheating on her husband. With me.

" . . . he just wants the money. Money that he's not entitled to, but I'm sure I'll write a hefty check. Are you still listening?" she asks with a smile, and then the smile fades when she gets a good look at my face. "Wyatt?"

"Let me get this straight. You're *not* legally divorced."

"Well, I was, but—"

"Answer me. It's a simple yes or no, Amelia."

"No." Her eyes narrow. "That's what's happening when I go to L.A. next week."

I lean on the countertop, hang my head, and do my best to not punch a wall.

"I fell in love with a fucking *married* woman."

"I don't understand—"

"Exactly. You don't understand. Amelia, I've told you that I love you. I have molded you into my life so completely, I can't even look around my house without seeing you there. And I *loved* that. I was *high* on it. I couldn't wait to have you there permanently. But now it's going to torment me for the rest of my fucking life."

"What are you talking—"

"I was ready to build a life with you." I pace away and stare out the glass door to the pool. "I was committed to you. Completely. I would have *died* to keep you safe."

"Why are you speaking in the past tense?"

I turn to look at her and see all of my hopes and dreams evaporate. "Because this was a deal-breaker for me from the beginning, and you fucking *knew* that, Amelia. You're not divorced."

"It's a technicality, Wyatt." She shakes her head and rubs her hand down her clean, naked face. "I *was* divorced, and he contested it. It's not like I have a lovesick husband sitting around somewhere. I didn't leave him yesterday."

"I don't care when you left him," I yell and turn away from her. "It doesn't matter when you left him. You didn't divorce him."

"Yes, I did."

I shake my head. "If it was as simple as a technicality, you would have told me, yet you managed to avoid that little piece of information for almost *two months*. Jesus, I've been inside you for two months."

"Don't you dare make our relationship out to be dirty."

"We don't have a relationship, Amelia. We've been committing adultery."

Her face goes red. "Get the fuck out of my house."

"Gladly." I walk past her, careful not to touch her. When I get to the door, I stop and look back at her. She hasn't turned around. "Did you do this on purpose? Were you just playing with me? Or did you think I wouldn't care?"

She spins, fury all over her face. "Get the fuck out!"

I nod and leave, shutting the door behind me, and get in my car. Rather than go home, I speed away, not sure where I'm going. I just know that I can't be close to her right now.

I'm numb. Every part of me is numb.

Well, every part but my heart. That seems to be a bloody mess. Unfortunately, Jace can't fix this one.

No one can fix it.

I've done the one thing that I swore I would *never* do. I started a relationship with a woman who was already tied to another man. I know what it is to be on the receiving end of that, and I wouldn't ever want to put anyone through that. It's agony.

It seems both sides are fucking agony.

I pull into Jace's driveway and bang on his door. He opens it, blinking sleep out of his eyes, and takes one look at me, scowls, and stands back, silently inviting me inside.

"What's wrong?" he asks immediately.

"She's married," I reply and pace his living room.

"I'm sorry, what?"

"Amelia is married."

"Not to you."

I laugh humorlessly and then look at him like he's an idiot. "You're still half asleep. No, not to me. If she were married to me, and yes, I'd planned that she would be at some point in the not so distant future, I wouldn't be standing here wanting to punch the fuck out of someone."

"Hey." He raises his hands in surrender. "Don't punch me. I don't even know what's going on."

I rub my hand over my mouth and walk to the window. Jace has a view of the city. People are driving, working. Living their lives.

And mine is falling apart.

"I loved her," I say. "Fuck me, I still love her, and she destroyed me with one sentence. 'So ready for my divorce to be final.'"

"I'm going to go out on a limb—precariously, by the way, because I don't want to get decked—and guess that you didn't know that."

I shake my head. "No. She said she was divorced."

I turn and look at Jace. "She said that? She didn't say separated?"

I shake my head again. "Not long after we met, we were having lunch, and she said she was divorced. You know me, man. I never would have pursued her if I knew she was still married to someone else."

"He's not here," he points out, and I just glare at him.

"Jace."

"I know. Jesus, Cruella did a number on you."

"And now Amelia is doing a number on someone else."

"Hey, you don't know that. Did you ask for specifics? Circumstances?"

"It doesn't matter." The fight is leaving me, and I'm just left with despair. "She's married, Jace. And that's a deal-breaker for me."

"It's a deal-breaker for most of us," he says softly. "I'm sorry, Wyatt."

"What is it with me and women?" I ask him. "That's not rhetorical, I'd really like an answer."

"You love hard," he says and then scratches the back of his head. "But I don't think you're blind. You want to believe the best in people, and you can't blame yourself for trusting."

"That's just it, I *don't* trust. Not easily."

"I know."

"But I trusted her."

"Yeah. You did."

eighteen

Amelia

Two days. It's been two damn days since the fiasco in the kitchen. I've cried.

Okay, let's be real, I'm still crying. I don't quite remember what my face looked like before. Now it's red, and my eyes are swollen with bruises around them. My lips are even puffy from blowing my nose so much.

I didn't know that could happen.

I also didn't know that my heart could hurt like this. Like someone has stabbed it a thousand times, and my chest is a bloody, gaping hole.

I love him, and I know that if he'd just listen to me, we could work this out.

But he won't answer me. I've texted a dozen times, I've called.

Shit, I even stood on his doorstep and knocked on the door for a good thirty minutes yesterday. His car was in the driveway. I sound like a crazy woman.

Yeah, not my finest hour.

He won't talk to me.

That might be what hurts most of all. He won't let me explain.

My doorbell rings, but there's no need to have false hope that it could be Wyatt. It's not.

I open the door, and Jace is standing there, looking so much like his brother that I start to cry again.

"Hey, hey, hey," he says as he steps inside and pulls me into a hug. "That's not the kind of reception a guy wants when a beautiful woman sees him."

"I'm not beautiful," I mumble into his chest. "I'm a fucking mess."

"Well, I didn't want to say anything, but yes. You're a mess." He grips my shoulders and pushes me back so he can look at me. His handsome face folds into a frown. "Seriously, Lia, you don't look good."

"This is what agony looks like," I inform him and walk away to sit on the couch. He follows and sits in a chair opposite me. "Have you talked to him?"

"A little," he confirms, and I can see in his eyes that he's not willing to say more.

"I know you're loyal to him, Jace. And I don't want to put you in the middle. I'm not asking you to deliver a message or anything like that."

"I am loyal to him," he confirms and leans forward, planting his elbows on his knees. "But you look like you could use a friend."

I nod, unable to speak as tears clog my throat again. I reach for a tissue and rub my already raw eyes. "My heart hurts." I cover my chest with my hand.

"I can't fix this," he says softly. "But do you want to talk?"

I nod again, but my throat is still closed. It seems all I can do is nod. "Give me a second."

"I'm not in a hurry."

I take a deep breath, blow my nose, and settle back on the couch, pulling my feet up under me. "I wasn't looking for him. Or anyone, for that matter."

I purge it all out. My separation from Vinnie, the divorce, my job, meeting Wyatt, and even most of our relationship. It all comes rushing out in a word vomit that I can't seem to control. But Jace just sits back and listens intently, his eyes narrowing now and then, but there's no judgment on his face as I tell him about falling in love with his brother and then receiving the letter a few days ago.

"We said horrible things," I continue. "And I made him get out. But I honestly don't think he would have listened to me in that moment anyway."

"I agree," he says but doesn't elaborate. "Wow, you fucked up, Amelia."

And queue the waterworks again. "I know it," I say. "But I didn't *mean* to. That's the point of all of this. I don't have a malicious bone in my damn body, and I certainly didn't mean to mislead him. I was too busy falling in love with him, feeling good about myself when I was with him to worry about Vinnie and the divorce. It's truly a technicality in my head. But Wyatt wouldn't listen."

"You know his past."

I nod and wipe my nose. "I just thought we were past the baggage. But we're not. And now he's gone. He won't talk to me, Jace. I've texted and called. I made a fool out of myself on his doorstep yesterday. And look at me." I hold my arms out. "I'm a disaster."

"You're still a beautiful disaster," he says with a small smile.

"You're just being nice. Because you're all so nice." I crumple again. "Seriously, I have to pull it together. I leave for L.A. tomorrow. I still have to pack my shit and sit in mediation in a week. Do you have any advice? Without giving away any confidences?"

He sighs, runs his hand through his hair the way Wyatt does, and then looks me in the eyes. "Get divorced, Lia. Finalize it, and give it time."

I shrug. "I'm not good at being patient."

"Well, you're going to have to be this time."

"Do you think I have a chance with him?"

"I think that you're both hurting, and some space will be good. I don't know what's going to happen, and that's the truth of it. Go to L.A. and get your affairs in order, then move on with your life."

"With or without him," I whisper. My eyes close, and tears escape down my cheeks. "I hope it's not without him."

"Either way, you're going to be fine, Lia. I know that."

I nod. "Thanks for coming by. You really did help. Maybe I just needed to talk about it all."

"You're welcome."

He stands, and I walk him to the door. As we walk to his car, Wyatt walks out of his house across the street. My heart soars for a moment.

God, even from far away he looks fantastic.

But when he sees us, he pauses and then laughs. There's no humor in his face. He shakes his head and doesn't say a word as he climbs into his car and drives away, not giving me another look.

"Fuck." My eyes well with tears again, and Jace wraps his arm around me in comfort.

"Give him time," he repeats and kisses the top of my head.

"THIS SUCKS," I mutter a week later as Pam and I wait for the mediator to come back into the room. Having separate conference rooms for this was absolutely the way to go. I don't want to see Vinnie.

I might deck him, and then he'd press charges, and I can't live my life from jail.

"It's not as bad as going back to court," she reminds me and makes notes in a folder that she's working on as we wait. Finally, after about thirty minutes, the mediator returns.

He's a kind-looking, older man, who worked in family law for many years and does mediation now.

I like him.

"We have a counteroffer," he says once he's seated. "But first, I have to ask. Was he always so *odd?*"

"Yeah." I swallow and push my hair off of my cheek. "He's not good at this stuff."

"No kidding. Okay, well, they've come back with this amount, paid in full." He slides a piece of paper across the table, and I jerk my gaze back up to him in surprise.

"Tell me this is a joke."

"No, it's not. You don't have to say yes. We can go back with another number."

I stare at Pam. "I already paid him a fair amount when we got divorced the first time. This is ridiculous."

"To be fair," the mediator says, "in the state of California, he's entitled to half of what you made when you were still together. The amount you paid him wasn't half."

"No, it wasn't," I agree. "Because he mocked me every day for my career. He *hated* it. He said my followers were stupid, and he didn't even want to be on the bank account because he didn't want to know anything about it."

"Yeah, he's claiming now that you hid money from him."

"That cocksucker," I mutter and stand to pace the room. "He was verbally abusive for *years*, told me to take my money and leave, and now he wants it. He doesn't care about me. He never did."

"You need to take your emotions out of this," Pam says sternly, her eyes shrewd. "I get that he's fucked you. I've seen it, too. But this is now a business transaction, Lia."

I take a deep breath and sit at the table, listening.

"You can decline everything today," she continues. "And then we'll go back to court. That can take months. Maybe even a year. A judge will most likely award him half anyway because that's the law in California. So, you can continue to pay legal fees and delay this further, or you can think like the businesswoman you are. We can end this. Today." She folds her hands on her folder. "And I'd like to remind you that you're about to launch a makeup brand. The money you're about to start bringing in is so much bigger than this. Don't ruin that for yourself. And don't give him an opportunity to get his hands on a piece of that, as well."

"I agree," the mediator says. "And I'm Switzerland."

I nod and look at the figure again. "I won't agree to his legal fees. He's the one who decided to take it this far."

"Agreed," Pam says and writes on the paper. "No legal fees. What about the money?"

"Let's go back with this." I write a smaller figure down. "And tell him I'll pay it in one lump sum rather than monthly payments. I want him *gone*. If he agrees, I'll write a check today."

He nods, picks up the paper, and leaves. Pam and I stare at each other for a long moment.

"How do you do this, day in and day out? Isn't it sad?"

"It can be," she says with a nod. "It can also be satisfying. There are people that leave situations far worse than yours."

"I suppose so," I reply. "I hadn't thought of that."

It's not long before the mediator returns with a smile. "They agree. Pam, you can draw up the papers, and he'll sign them."

"He also needs to sign something that says he can't ever come back at me, wanting more money."

"Of course," Pam says with a nod. "You write that check, and I'll draw up the paperwork. We'll file these with the court this afternoon, and you'll officially be divorced in fourteen days."

I reach for my checkbook and feel physically ill as I write out the check, then slide it to the middle of the table. It's an obscene amount of money, but if it's the cost of getting Vinnie out of my life for good, it's worth every penny.

In less than an hour, the papers are all signed, Vinnie has my check, and we're done.

"Thank you," I say to Pam and give her a hug. "Seriously, thank you for everything."

"You're welcome." She pulls back. "Next time, get a prenup."

"There won't be a next time," I say with a laugh. "No way, no how."

"Never say never," she says with a wink. I follow her out of the room and turn to leave her offices, and there he is ahead of me, facing me. Vinnie.

His eyebrows climb, and then his face transforms into a smirk.

And I feel nothing at all. I just turn and leave, without a word. It's time to get on with my life.

"WHEN WILL YOU be home?" Archer asks a week later. I'm walking around my now-empty apartment, waiting for the landlord to show up for a walk-through so I can hand in my keys.

"In a few days," I reply. My voice echoes in the empty space. "The truck should be in Seattle tomorrow with my things."

"I've already talked to the truck driver, and I'll meet him at the house. I have all of that covered. Are you okay to drive up by yourself?"

"I'm not. Anastasia is flying down tomorrow morning. I have one last meeting in the afternoon, and then we're hitting the road."

"She didn't say anything," he says. "How did everything go?"

"Well, he got a lot of money, but not as much as he wanted, which I'm going to call a win. I didn't pay his legal fees."

"Damn right, you didn't. You should have let me beat him up when I wanted to."

I laugh. "Trust me, it's not that I didn't want to. But it's over. The divorce will be final in a few days, I'll be in Seattle, and I don't ever have to deal with him again."

"How are things with Wyatt?"

"Non-existent," I reply softly and walk a circle in my old kitchen. "I haven't spoken to him in two weeks. And, frankly, I think I'm going to just move on, Archer. I tried, and he didn't want to listen. I won't beg."

"No. You're not one who begs, Lia. No one is worth that."

"Nope."

"How did your meetings go? Are they okay with you commuting from Seattle?"

"So far, it isn't an issue. I had a photo shoot yesterday." I stroll down the hallway to my bedroom and walk slowly to the window. I can see a lot of the city from here. "I liked this condo. I felt so proud and independent when I rented it after I left Vinnie."

"It was a great transition home," he says, and it's like a lightbulb turns on.

"That's a good way to describe it," I reply. "You're really smart some-times. Is that why they let you own the company?"

He chuckles. "You're starting to get some of your sass back."

Sass.

That's what Wyatt says before . . . *no.* Turn it off.

My doorbell rings.

"The landlord is here. I'd better go. If there are any issues tomorrow, just let me know."

"There won't be," he says. "Keep me posted on your drive, and be safe. Love you."

"Love you."

I blink away tears as I hurry to the door and open it wide. Maria, the little landlord that I've worked with for more than two years, smiles at me. "Hello, Lia."

"Hello, Maria." She walks in and glances about.

"I'm so sad that you're leaving," she says. She has a clipboard tucked in her arm and smiles up at me. She's a petite, kind woman. "We don't always get tenants as good as you."

"Well, I loved living here," I assure her. "Where would you like to start?"

We spend the next thirty minutes walking through the unit. I get docked for three nail holes that I don't have time to fill and paint, but otherwise, the condo is as I found it.

I hand her the keys and walk out to my car, happy to finally have it back. Not that I wasn't grateful for Jules' car, but there's something to be said for being surrounded by your own things.

I drive to the hotel, give the car to the valet, and plan to soak in the bathtub for a while then order room service before crashing for the night.

My room is a suite on one of the highest floors with an ocean view. I figured since I was wrapping up my divorce and I'd be here for a while getting my stuff packed and attending meetings, I'd splurge a little.

Once I'm out of the bath, I pull on some black yoga pants and an oversized sweatshirt that hangs over one shoulder. I'm just about to call room service when the room phone rings.

"Hello?"

"Miss Montgomery, this is Ron at the front desk. We have a visitor for you."

Could it be?

"Who is it, please?"

"Anastasia Montgomery."

Silly.

I grin, excited to see her. "Send her up."

Of course, it's not Wyatt. He doesn't want me. And the sooner I come to accept that, the better.

Anastasia knocks on the door, and I rush to open it, then throw my arms around her and pull her into the room.

"You're here!"

"Regretting it already," she says, her voice strained. "Can't breathe."

"I'm so happy to see you." I kiss her cheek before she jerks out of my grasp.

"Ugh." She wipes my kiss off of her cheek but smiles at me. "Surprise."

"I thought you were coming tomorrow." I clap my hands excitedly and dance a little jig.

"And I thought you could probably use the company." She pulls her handbag off her shoulder and wiggles out of her sweatshirt. "It's hot in L.A."

"I'm so happy."

She immediately holds up her hands. "Do *not* death squeeze me again."

"Can I kiss you?"

"No."

"Spoilsport." I laugh and pull her bag inside, stowing it next to the closet. "I was just about to order room service. Are you hungry?"

"Hungry and grimy from the flight. Is this the only bed?"

"Yeah," I say. "Choose something to eat, and then you can shower while I order food."

"Does this mean we're sleeping together again?"

"Of course. Seriously, though, look at the menu. I'm starving."

She narrows her eyes at me menacingly. "I'm not snuggling with you."

"Of course, you are. What do you want?"

"I should have stayed home."

"You love me."

She laughs and takes a quick look at the menu. "I'll have the five-hundred-dollar kid's cheeseburger. Jesus, why is room service so expensive?"

"That might be an exaggeration. I'll get you the five-thousand-dollar big person's cheeseburger." I laugh and shoo her into the bathroom. "Enjoy your shower, and I'll order. And, Stasia?"

"Yeah."

"Thank you. I'm seriously happy that you're here."

"You're welcome. I want the two-thousand-dollar onion rings, too."

"Done."

nineteen

Wyatt

There's a moving truck parked in Amelia's driveway. I don't know if she's over there. I haven't seen her.

Not that I've been looking for her. If anything, I've been avoiding any and all reminders of her. Not that it helps to dull the ache that's set up permanent residence in my chest.

Almost three weeks without her has been torture that I don't wish on my worst enemy. But I have to learn to get over it because, otherwise, it's going to be a very long, painful life.

I grab my keys and walk out to my car. I'm meeting Jace and Levi for lunch. Before I can climb into the vehicle, I hear my name being called from across the street.

"Wyatt!" It's Archer, jogging toward me. He doesn't look like he's going to take a swing at me.

Yet.

I don't say anything, I just wait for him to join me.

"I'm going to cut to the chase," he says. "You should cut her a break."

"She lied."

He rolls his eyes and pulls his phone out of his back pocket, scrolling. "Here. These are photos from her *divorce* party, months before she even met you."

I take the phone and scroll through photos of a smiling Amelia. She's holding a cake that says *HAPPY DIVORCE.*

"She was divorced, man. She even has signed papers from the court. Then the asshole contested it, and some jerk judge decided to entertain it. I'm not going to tell you everything because that's her story to tell, but I have a feeling that she tried to explain, and you weren't ready to hear it."

"It doesn't change the fact that she was married when I met her, and she didn't tell me. Even knowing the way I feel about marriage, she didn't say anything."

Archer holds up his hands. "All I'm saying is give her a chance to talk before you decide to cut her off for good. And now, I'm out of it. Good luck, man."

He jogs back over to the truck, and I climb into my car.

She did text and call, and I didn't respond. There wasn't anything to say that hadn't already been said.

I quickly scroll through her texts. It's mostly, *please talk to me.*

There's one voicemail that I haven't listened to. I hit play.

Hey, it's me. Again. I can't get you to talk to me, so I'm going to try to quickly explain some things in this voicemail. I don't know how long I can talk before it cuts me off, but here I go.

I didn't intentionally lie to you, Wyatt. I am divorced, and I can show you the papers if you want to see them. Vinnie contested because he wasn't happy with the settlement amount. I've made a lot of money in the past few years, and he thought he should have more, even though he'd been verbally abusive and mean to me for a long time. He hated my job, like I told you.

Anyway, months after the divorce was final, I got a letter saying that it wasn't final, and that we'd be going back to court. I met with my attorney, and she recommended I get out of L.A. for a while so she could handle the legal stuff.

And then I met you.

And I fell in love with you.

She sniffles.

I was so happy and busy being with you that I never even thought about Vinnie and his stupid contest case. It had been such a long and difficult divorce that I was just happy to be with my family and with this amazing man who loved me back, the way I deserve to be loved.

I do love you, Wyatt. But I'm going to leave you be now because you clearly don't want to hear from me. All I ask is, if you cared for me even a little bit, please let me talk to you in person so I can apologize and explain. Please don't let this be something that he takes from me, too.

Okay. Bye.

The message ends, and I blow out a breath and toss my phone onto the seat next to me. Am I being stubborn? Ridiculous?

Is there a grey area here?

I start the car and drive to the restaurant where I'm meeting my brothers. They're both already there, and there's a beer waiting for me.

"I need this." I take a long sip.

"You still look like shit," Jace says.

"Thanks. I feel like shit."

"Have you seen her?" Levi asks.

"Do we have to talk about this? Don't either of you have something else to discuss? A woman? Work? Something?"

"I don't," Jace says and looks at Levi. "You?"

"Nope, I'm good."

"You both suck." I sigh. "No, I haven't seen her. I have no idea what's going on with her. Because she fucking lied to me."

But for the first time, doubt has planted itself in my head.

"What are you thinking?" Levi asks. I tell them about my encounter with Archer, and the voicemail from Amelia.

"Huh," Jace says.

"So, she doesn't necessarily have a lovesick husband pining away for her," Levi points out.

"And she's most likely divorced now. Again," Jace adds.

"Yes."

I drink more of my beer.

"You know," Jace begins, "you keep punishing her for Cruella's fuck-ups. Maybe you shouldn't be together."

I narrow my eyes at him, but he keeps talking.

"I'm not saying that to be a dick. You know I saw Lia a few days after it all went down, and she told me quite a bit. I think she needed to explain it all to *someone*, and you wouldn't hear her."

I swallow, guilt sitting heavily in my stomach.

"And I think Cruella really fucked you up, man," Jace continues. "I get it, she's a selfish bitch, and what she pulled isn't cool. But Lia isn't her. And she may have screwed up, but she wants to make it right."

"I fucked up," I say and drain the last of my beer.

"I think you both fucked up," Levi says.

"I wouldn't listen to her. I didn't let her talk."

"Okay, you fucked up more," he replies with a shrug.

"If you're going to keep punishing her for what your ex did, you don't deserve her," Jace says. "Because that shit isn't fair."

"She knew from the beginning how I felt about marriage and infidelity," I reply. "I was always honest about that."

"And in her head, she was divorced," Levi replies. "Because she was. And the ex was being a jerk and making it harder for her."

"I get it," Jace adds with a shrug. "I would flip my shit if I was in love with someone and I found out she was still legally married."

"Oh, yeah," Levi agrees. "I might kill someone. I can make it look like an accident."

"But now that you're cooled off, maybe it's time to listen to her," Jace says.

"You know, we always think of you as the class clown," I say to Jace. "But I guess that Ivy League education did its job."

"I'm smarter than I look," he says proudly. "I have certificates and everything."

"You're such a dork," Levi says with a laugh.

"I need to talk to her," I say and then sigh. "I hope it's not too late."

"All you can do is try," Levi says.

"I'm leaving. Sorry, guys, I don't want to wait."

"Go."

I rush out of the restaurant and to my car. The drive home is longer than I'd like and seems to take forever.

The moving truck is gone now, and the house is quiet. I park in my own driveway and hurry over to her front door. I ring the bell and wait.

Nothing.

I ring it again and knock.

Still nothing.

Frustrated, I walk around the house, but there's no movement inside, just boxes stacked all over the place.

I return to the front door and pound on it one more time in case she's upstairs or something.

Just as I'm about to leave, Natalie and Jules pull into the driveway.

"What do you want?" Jules asks as they approach me.

"Where's Amelia?"

"She's not here," Jules replies, and Natalie rolls her eyes.

"She's still in L.A.," Nat says.

"What the hell, Nat?" Jules demands.

"This is none of our business, and you went through something very similar and, well, it worked out for you, didn't it?"

"Still." Jules glares at me. "Okay, I hate it when she's right."

"When will she be back?" I ask Natalie.

"In a few days," she replies and props her hands on her hips, studying me.

"How much do you know?"

"Enough to know that you're kind of a dick," Jules says, and I can only hang my head and laugh ruefully.

"Yeah, I've been a bit of a dick."

"No, I'd say a big dick. A giant ol' dick." She crosses her arms over her chest. "And contrary to popular belief, women don't like a giant dick. And I don't like that you made Lia cry, you insensitive ass."

"I mean, there were two of us there, so I don't think this is *all* my fault."

"No, she was dumb, too. But you're not my cousin, so I'm really pissed off at you." She steps to me and pushes her finger into my chest. "You fucked with someone I love, Wyatt Crawford."

"What would you like for me to do?"

I don't flick her finger off of me or even move. She's on fire.

"Fix it," she says simply and backs up. "You need to fucking fix it."

"I'd like to."

Natalie's smiling in that serene way she does. I swear, she's the calmest person I've ever met in my life.

"It's going to work out," she says with a nod. "Now, we have to meet with the insurance adjuster really quick regarding my studio. Lia will be here in a few days."

"Thanks."

I turn to walk away, but Jules steps in front of me, scowling. "Don't fuck it up, Wyatt. I like you."

"Despite the fact that I'm a giant dick?"

"I think we can work with that."

She walks away, and I laugh as I saunter back to my house. I haven't felt this hopeful in more than two weeks.

I pull out my phone and decide to send Amelia a quick text.

Hey. Drive safely home. I'd like to see you when you get here.

My thumb hovers for a moment, and then I decide . . . fuck it.

I love you.

I hit send.

twenty

Amelia

"This passenger seat is comfy." We've been on the road for a few hours, and Anastasia offered to drive for the first leg since my head was still full of information from my business meetings. "Do you want snacks yet?"

"No. Did you happen to notice that your snacks look like a seven-year-old was set free in the candy and chip aisle with a hundred bucks?"

"As it should be on a road trip," I reply with a laugh. "Road trips are for junk food."

"For someone getting over a man, you sure are eating a lot. When I'm sad, I don't eat anything at all."

"I'm the opposite. I eat everything in sight. I can't help it." I sigh and open a can of Pringles, then pop a sour cream and onion chip into my mouth. "These are my favorite."

"Tell me what they said in your meeting."

"Okay." I swallow and take a drink of my orange soda. "They showed me the photographs that we took the other day, and they actually turned out really great. They emailed them to me, so I'll pull them up and show you in a minute. They're putting together a full campaign, and get this: Sephora wants to exclusively sell all of the products."

"Shut the fuck up," she says, staring at me in awe. "As in, the Sephora in pretty much every mall in America?"

"That's the one." I nod and feel tears prick my eyes again. "This is big, girl. Like, bigger than anything I could have imagined. YouTube made me a millionaire, but this . . . This could make me wealthier than I ever thought possible."

"Goddamn it, you're going to make me cry," she says and wipes at her eye. "Seriously, Lia, this is so damn great. When will we be able to buy it in the store?"

"If all goes well, next month." I pass her a tissue and keep one to dab my own eyes. "I'll do a small tour, showing up at stores to do makeup tutorials and sign headshots."

"Wow," she says, shaking her head. "My sister is way cooler than me. And I'm totally okay with that."

I laugh and lean over to kiss her cheek. She doesn't even rub it off this time.

"We will have to throw a party when it launches in Seattle."

"You'll need cake," she says excitedly. "So just tell me when, and I'll clear those days so I'm only making a cake for you. And Nic can cover the cupcakes."

"Yesss, that'll be awesome. You could decorate it with little lipsticks and eyeshadow palates that look like Amelia Cosmetics."

"This is gonna be fun," she replies with a little shimmy just as my phone pings with a text.

"Holy shit. Wyatt just texted me."

She glances at me in surprise. "Well, read it. Aloud."

I read his message to myself first. If I weren't in the car, I would have come out of my seat. "Are you fucking kidding me?"

"That's what he said?"

"No." I read it to her. "*Now* he's concerned? *Now*, he wants to throw *I love you* around? What a jerk. I'm blocking his number."

"You know, you guys are a bit too much drama for me," Stasia says with a yawn.

"I tried to talk to him for *days*. I tried everything, Anastasia. And he was having none of it. And now, out of nowhere, he sends me this? As if nothing has happened? What kind of mind game is he playing here?"

"And these are the days of our lives," she mutters, shifting in her seat. "Call him and ask him, Lia. Because I don't have the answer to any of those questions."

"Why are you such a bitch?" I demand, giving her the stink eye and shoving about four chips into my mouth. "This is why I don't tell you things."

She laughs and then shakes her head at me. "I'm being honest. I agree, it's weird that he's texting you out of the blue. How does he even know that you're driving back today?"

"I don't know." I frown. "Who's he talking to?"

"Call the man."

"I already blocked his number."

"Unblock it and call him. You wanted him to talk, well, he's talking."

"No." I toss my phone into my handbag and reach for another chip. "I know, I'm being stupid, but that pissed me off. I'm not texting him *or* calling him."

"Well, then stop talking about him because it's really annoying."

"We should drive through wine country," I say, changing the subject. Mostly, I want to get my mind off of Wyatt. I'd already decided that I'm moving forward without him, and damn it, I'm sticking to that. I don't care if he's tall and sexy with the most tender hazel eyes I've ever seen. Or if his hair feels like silk in my fingers. Or if he makes me feel smart and clever when we talk for hours on end.

I can do this without him.

"I thought you wanted to get home as soon as possible," she replies, reaching for some of my Pringles. "The fastest route is to stick to the freeway."

"Yeah, you're right. I have a bunch of unpacking and avoiding a sexy man ahead of me."

"Are you going to be able to live in that house with him right across the street?"

I frown and drink more orange soda. "Of course. I'm a grown woman. I don't have to look at him. I'll avoid him."

No, I'm not sure I'll be okay. But I'm going to do my best.

"Uh-huh." She rolls her eyes. "Good luck with that."

I DON'T KNOW if I've ever felt exhaustion on this level. Even after I left Vinnie, I don't think I was this weary.

Jules and Anastasia just left after spending all last night helping me unpack my boxes. Anastasia still hasn't been home since we pulled into my driveway yesterday afternoon.

Instead, we called Jules, and she came over to help us plow through the boxes and get most of everything situated so I can get back to regular life again. I owe them both, big time.

Perhaps a shopping trip is in our near future. I'll reward all of our hard work.

I grin, plant my hands on my hips, and gaze around the space. It feels *amazing* to have my own things here, mingled with a few of the pieces that Jules and Nate bought months ago when I first arrived.

And now that they're gone, and the bulk of the work is finished, I'm not entirely sure what to do with myself.

I glance into the kitchen, and to the pool area beyond, and feel a grin spread across my face.

Check that. I *do* know what I want to do.

I hurry and pour a glass of tea, reach into the fridge and grab my cucumber eye mask. I pull an ice pack out of the freezer and carry everything to my favorite chaise lounge by the water.

It's late enough in the day that most of the patio is in the shade so I don't have to worry about getting too much sun. I can totally nap right here if I want.

And trust me, *I want.*

I take a sip of the cold tea, then settle back on the lounge with the ice pack against the back of my neck. I lay the cucumber mask over my eyes and let my body relax into the chair, soaking up the quiet. The calm.

It's absolute heaven.

I'm just drifting to sleep when I hear the doorbell. I know it's not my family; I've already spoken to most of them this morning. Anastasia just went home to crash.

No, I know who it is.

And he and his sexy doorbell can just fuck right off.

Wait, it's *my* doorbell. I clearly need a nap.

I'm just about to fall asleep again when I hear his footsteps coming onto the patio.

"I don't know why he thinks he can just walk onto my property, like I want to see him," I mutter aloud, not moving.

"God, you're fucking beautiful," he says, his voice gruff.

"I blocked your number. I can't hear you," I reply. If I let him stay, if I look at him, I'll want him. I'll soften and want him to stay, not just for today, but for *always*. And he hurt me.

My God, he hurt me.

"Are you going to give me a chance to speak with you?" he asks, and I frown.

"Doesn't feel good when the shoe is on the other foot, does it?"

"Amelia, look at me."

I sit up and let the mask fall to my lap, the ice to the seat of the chair, and scowl at him.

Fucking hell, he looks amazing. His hair is a mess, his face scruffy, and it looks like he hasn't slept in a week.

"Who do you think you are?" I demand and stand so I can look him square in the eye. It seems that despite my exhaustion, I'm not too tired for this.

Because I *need* to stand up for myself.

"I tried to talk to you for *days* to explain everything, and you wouldn't listen. You wouldn't reply. It was like beating my head against a brick wall."

"I know," he says and shoves his hands into his pockets, his eyes hungrily eating me up. "I fucked up, Amelia."

"Yeah. You did." I turn away and stand at the edge of the pool, watching a leaf float on the water. "I don't even know where to start with you. You say you want me to talk to you, but how can I when I'm afraid that I'll say the wrong thing, and you'll just get pissed and leave again?"

"I'm here, and I'm not leaving," he says. He's moved closer to me, and chills ripple down my back. "I listened to your voicemail."

"When?" I whirl around and cross my arms over my chest. "When did you listen to it?"

"The other day. When I texted you."

I tilt my head to the side. "You waited *two weeks* from when I left it to listen?"

"I was having a . . . rough time."

"Yeah? Well, me too. Let me lay this out for you, Wyatt. The man that I loved, who claimed to love me too, decided he was so angry at me that he wouldn't let me anywhere near him. You shut me out completely, without a word. Without a chance. And now *you* want a chance."

My God, I want to run into his arms and make all of this hurt go away. He's like a freaking magnet to my heart.

"I need a chance," he replies with a nod. His voice is still soft. He sighs, the muscle in his jaw clenching as he seemingly pulls his thoughts together. "I had an inexcusable knee-jerk reaction. That's the best way to describe it. Lia, when I heard you say that you weren't divorced yet, it cut me at the knees. I was the victim of adultery, and I would *never* do that to someone else."

"I hate that word when you use it in regards to us," I reply. "Because that's not what we did."

"I see that now," he says with a nod. "And I apologize for ever imply-ing that that's what it is."

"Was," I correct him. "Because we don't have anything now."

He blinks rapidly, watching me with eyes full of heartache, and I want to pull the words back. Except, they aren't untrue.

"This isn't love, Wyatt. Accusations and the silent treatment? Not listening and talking through issues? That's *not* love. And I'll be damned if I do that again because I deserve to be loved."

"You *are* loved, damn it."

"Am I?" I prop my hands on my hips now. "Let's say we work this out, and we are together. I'll always be afraid of saying the wrong thing, or making a mistake and having you walk out the door again." Tears fill my eyes, and I brush at them impatiently, feeling the hurt surround my heart at the memory of it all. "I couldn't survive it twice."

"I'm so sorry." He pushes his hands through his hair and paces in a circle. "Jesus, I want to reach for you so badly my body aches with it."

"Don't touch me." I hug my arms around myself and shake my head slowly. "I can't have you touch me."

"Amelia, I fucked up so big. I get it. It's all I can think about. I miss you."

He swallows hard, and I can't look away from him. My tongue is glued to the roof of my mouth, and all I can do is listen.

"You set my soul on fire. Does that sound cheesy?" He smiles softly. "I didn't know that the fire was gone until I met you, and it was like I was in the middle of an inferno. You gave me a new purpose every day. Every. Day.

"I was so afraid to love you, to *really* give you all of my love because love had hurt me in the past—"

"Love didn't hurt you," I interrupt him. His hands fall to his sides. "Someone incapable of loving you, hurt you. Don't get it twisted, Wyatt. This is something I've had to learn myself."

"You're right," he says with a nod. "I hadn't thought of it that way."

"I can't be punished for her lack of love," I reply softly. "I need someone fearless in their love for me. Someone who is more afraid of losing me than of the possibility of being hurt."

"That's accurate," he says with a nod. "We both deserve that. And, Lia, you have it. I wish I could adequately explain this to you, so I'm going to try. I get lost in you, in the best way there is. I look into your eyes, and I see myself there. I see my own feelings shining back at me, and that's completely new to me.

"Your voice gives me butterflies. Your touch ignites every nerve ending in my body. And when we're together, well, it's the closest to heaven that I'll ever be, I'll tell you that. I look at you, and I just love you. I love you so much that it terrifies me, and fills me with so much joy I think I might die from it.

"I'm *so sorry* for the way I acted, and I feel like a complete fool for not listening, for not *working* with you through it. It's the biggest regret and mistake of my life, and I'm standing here, baring my soul to you, praying that it's not too late to make it all right again. I need you, Amelia. I need you every fucking day of my life."

I chew on my lip, tears streaming down my cheeks. If this right here isn't love, I don't know what is.

"We have to work on it. This is going to be the most important job of our lives, Wyatt."

He swallows hard.

"Does this mean that you'll give me another chance?"

I nod, and I'm suddenly caught up in his arms, being swung around and hugged tighter than I ever have been.

"I thought I'd lost you," he says and sets me on my feet, framing my face in his hands and staring intently into my eyes. "It almost killed me."

"You broke me," I admit softly as he brushes a tear with his thumb. "I don't know that I've felt pain like that before, Wyatt. I need you to promise that it won't happen again."

"Never." His voice is firm and sure. "I'll never intentionally hurt you, my love."

"And I would never hurt you, either. You need to trust and remember that when you feel insecure or worried."

"I know."

He tips his forehead to mine.

"I'm so relieved that you're home."

I smile and grip his wrists in my hands. "Guess what?"

"What?"

"That technicality that almost ended us? It's done. As of yesterday, I'm a divorced woman."

"Thank Christ." He crushes his mouth to mine and lifts me effortlessly into his arms, carrying me to my chaise lounge and sits with me in his lap. "The idea of him still being tied to you made me homicidal."

"No need for that," I assure him and rest my head on his shoulder. "I have something else to tell you, and we might as well do this now in case it's another deal-breaker."

"Okay."

He doesn't even tense up under me.

"Not worried?"

"I don't think I have any more deal-breakers where you're concerned but go ahead."

I reach for my phone and bring up the photos from the shoot earlier in the week. "I've done well with my career, Wyatt. I make a good living and can afford things that make me happy. But I'm about to become a very wealthy woman."

I show him the photos, the campaign plans for the brand, the contract with Sephora's branding at the top.

"Why in the hell would this be a deal-breaker?"

"Because maybe you don't want to be a with a woman who earns more money than you."

He snorts. "Sweetheart, your job doesn't affect my job. The fact that this is happening for you is so fucking amazing and wonderful, and the product of your own hard work. I'll be happy to support you and help you in any way I can."

He kisses my forehead.

"And you should know, I do pretty well myself."

"I know, and I'm proud of you, too. So proud." I sit up so I can look into his eyes. "I think you're brilliant and amazing."

"Thank you." His lips twitch. "I'm not an asshole. Make millions. Buy all the things that you want. Quit your job tomorrow and become a tomato farmer for all I care. As long as I get to be standing next to you through all of it, I'm the happiest man in the world."

"I love you." I kiss him and nuzzle into him again. "I'm finally home."

twenty-one

Amelia

Three months later . . .

"**C**ome with me."

I sigh as I finish breaking down a box and throw it on the pile by the front door. "I'm so damn tired of moving. It's exhausting, and I'm over it."

"I know. We're almost finished." He pulls me to him and kisses me in that way he does when he's feeling particularly in the mood.

"I don't have time for hanky-panky," I say, pushing against his chest, but not too hard. I don't want him to let go, after all. "And I'm sweaty. That's not sexy."

"You're always sexy," he says and kisses the tip of my nose. "And I have something for you."

"You already renovated one of the bedrooms for my studio space and made room for all of my stuff. You've done a lot."

"And I'll keep doing it," he says as if it's really that simple. The past three months have been great. The misunderstandings have been few and easily worked through. It seems that those few weeks apart taught us both a few important lessons. "Now, come on."

He takes my hand and leads me out the back door to the grass where he has a big blanket spread out and a picnic set up.

"Lunch," he says simply. "And I need to talk to you about something."

"God, I'm hungry. You know, you have good timing with food."

"I'm glad you approve." He passes me a sandwich, and I dive in. "So, where we're currently sitting."

"Mm-hmm." I nod and look around, still loving the view of the water. "What about it?"

"It's about to become a pool."

I stop chewing and stare at him. "Come again?"

"I'm having a pool dug tomorrow. And this whole area will be patio space with a great area for you to relax and enjoy."

I set my food aside and climb into his lap. "I love you, you know that, right?"

"I hope so." His hands glide up and down my bare back. I'm wearing a sundress that dips low in the back, and his hands feel amazing. "I take it this means that you're happy with the pool idea?"

"So happy." I kiss his cheeks. "The pool was the only thing that made me sad about leaving Nat's house."

"I know," he replies and smiles when I raise an eyebrow. "You loved that space, but I'm relieved that you love me more."

"Well, yeah. There are perks to being with you."

"And now you'll have your pool."

My face sobers as he pulls my dress up around my waist and cups my naked ass in his hands. "Thank you."

"You're welcome."

I move against him and feel his hardness straining through his jeans.

"This seems like it might be uncomfortable."

His lips twitch.

"Maybe I should help you with it," I continue and bite his lower lip.

"That would be helpful," he says and leans back so I can unzip his pants and free him, jacking him. He sucks in a breath, hissing through his teeth. "Fucking hell, Amelia."

"I'm fond of your cock." I say it as though I'm making conversation about the weather. I rub my thumb over the tip, spreading the bead of precum around, and then, without further ado, I rise up and lower myself over him, making us both moan.

I rock, feeling him easily slide in and out, and it's not long before we're both a panting, heaving, sweaty mess, right in the backyard.

"Sorry that was such a quickie," I say, trying to catch my breath. "Clearly, you do things to me."

"Can't talk," he replies. "Dead."

"You can't die." I laugh and bite his chin, then roll off him and pat his cheeks. "Wake up. I need you."

"For my pool."

"That's one of the things," I confirm and reach for my sandwich again. "Thank you. For all of it."

"I'm not done yet."

I frown. "Seriously, if you say you've bought me an island, I'm going to say you've gone too far. This is a lot, Wyatt."

He readjusts himself and reaches in the picnic basket, pulling out a tiny, red box.

The kind of red box from Cartier that usually holds a girl's best friend.

"You are the best part of my life," he begins as he rises up on one knee, holding the box in front of him, and here I am, holding a fucking sandwich.

I set it aside, again, and swallow quickly as he keeps talking.

"You challenge me, make me laugh, and frankly, you're everything to me, Amelia. Will you please do me the absolute honor of becoming my wife? Build a life with me. Marry me."

He opens the box, revealing a stunning round diamond ring. But it's his eyes that I can't look away from.

"I love you so much," I say.

"Is that a yes?"

I laugh and hold out my hand, giddy as he slides the ring onto my finger, and then launch myself into his arms.

"That's a yes times a million, Wyatt Crawford."

The End